———————— ★ ————————

"I DON'T LIKE BRIBES. IF I WANTED MONEY THAT MUCH, I'D BE IN ANOTHER BUSINESS."

He hit the double fifteen with his first dart. "Shot. You could be badly hurt, Shaw. What's worth it?"

"What's worth so much to you?"

I shot again to start with a double six. I'm stubborn. This time I hit with my second dart, added 20, off at 269.

"Even your wife could be hurt," he said. "I'd hate to see anything happen to such a beautiful, talented lady."

I said, "You must be new at this. A lame con, a heavy-handed ⬚⬚⬚⬚ d threats that are sure to ⬚⬚⬚⬚⬚ d if you or eith⬚⬚ ⬚⬚⬚ on my ⬚⬚⬚

I⬚⬚⬚ ⬚⬚⬚ ts.

"N⬚⬚ ⬚⬚t three single twe⬚⬚ ⬚ance. "You would be dead⬚ ⬚ore you ever reached me."

———————— ★ ————————

DEADLY INNOCENTS

Also by MARK SADLER

THE FALLING MAN
HERE TO DIE
MIRROR IMAGE
CIRCLE OF FIRE

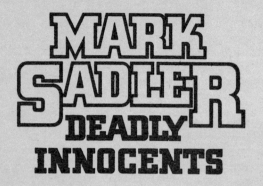

MARK SADLER
DEADLY INNOCENTS

WORLDWIDE.

TORONTO • NEW YORK • LONDON • PARIS
AMSTERDAM • STOCKHOLM • HAMBURG
ATHENS • MILAN • TOKYO • SYDNEY

DEADLY INNOCENTS

A Worldwide Mystery/August 1988

Published by arrangement with Walker and Company.

ISBN 0-373-26014-8

Printed in U.S.A.

For Francis M. (Mike) Nevins
booklover and true critic

ONE

THE DEAD MAN hung from a hook between two mops and a long net bag of toilet-paper rolls. By the collar of an army field jacket soaked with blood. Denim jeans, a work shirt, heavy black leather boots. The floor of the maintenance closet pooled with blood. A slim young man of average height. An ordinary face with a coarse handsomeness that came mostly from youth, and neat blond hair worn long but not quite touching his collar.

Mildred held out a bloody business card. "Mr. Shavitz found it on the closet floor."

It was ours: *Thayer, Shaw and Delaney—Security and Investigations: New York, Los Angeles.* I'm Paul Shaw. John Thayer and I work out of New York, but Dick Delaney needed help. Thayer is senior partner, so I flew out. The card had today's date and *4:00 P.M.* written on it.

We'd found our client.

"The police?" Mildred said.

Small and overweight, a native Angeleno as quick and blunt as any New Yorker, she's been Delaney's secretary since we opened shop. Thayer says she's too soft for our business, becomes emotional about the clients. He's told Dick that, but Dick runs his own office. Thayer says Dick is too soft. Thayer is single and wears steel-rimmed glasses. Soft or not, Mildred's worked for us a long time and knows the job. She wouldn't call the police until I was ready.

"A couple of minutes," I said.

Shavitz, the building manager, lit a cigarette, said nothing as I began to search the body. We were good tenants.

Our Los Angeles office is off Wilshire Boulevard in Hollywood. The glass double doors into the lobby of the building are identical to those leading into our Madison Avenue building, and there the resemblance ends. In New York it's a skyscraper; in Hollywood four stories and balconies. In New York, walls and masses. In Los Angeles, space and distance, except for the few tall buildings like distant islands in a sea of haze.

I'd flown out under protest: "Maureen has to stay in New York," I told Thayer. "You go west."

"A detective should never marry," Thayer said. "Especially not a woman with a career."

"You've mentioned that before."

"I expect I'll mention it again. The best flight to L.A. leaves at nine A.M."

Mildred met me at LAX in a company car. "A new client, due in the office at four this afternoon. You've got time to check in at our hotel, have a shower and a beer."

Our Hollywood hotel is also off Wilshire. A secluded hotel with suites instead of rooms, and an elite lobby cocktail lounge where deals are made. For business or pleasure. A three-star French restaurant hidden away, and a guests-only bar on the top floor with a sweeping view of the city and the distant Pacific on the two clear winter days of every year.

"Robert Peterson, but Dick thinks the name's a phony," Mildred filled me in as we drove. "The guy stumbled over the last name when he gave it, hesitated as if he had to think about what name he was using. He called for the appointment three days ago. He sounded young and nervous. Maybe scared. He was exact about the day and the time. It had to be today at four. He spoke low, as if he didn't want to be heard."

"Anything about what the problem is?"

"No."

"Address? Phone number? Job?"

"Nothing, Paul."

I took the shower, skipped the beer, and walked back to the office. The September heat had been pushing a hundred when I landed. Now, close to 4:00 P.M., it was already down to the seventies. By eight it would be cool enough for a sweater.

In Delaney's office I practiced my reassuring smile, and four o'clock came and went.

By four-thirty I wished I'd had the beer.

By five-thirty I needed more than a beer.

"If he shows by six," I told Mildred on my way out, "send him around to La Tolteca. At six, go home."

"Seven," she said. "He sounded awfully anxious."

La Tolteca specializes, of course, in margaritas, but they make a good enough Scotch and soda. My first went down fast. It's a long day when you fly New York to L.A. With the second I began to think about some dinner. By seven-thirty I thought about flying back to New York and Maureen.

"Mr. Shaw?"

He was a tall man in a rumpled brown suit. I'd seen him come in, look around, and then walk toward me with a weary step, as if he'd been on his feet all day. He wasn't young, and he didn't seem particularly scared or nervous, only tired.

"Your secretary told me I'd find you here."

Mildred was much too soft. He was already walking back toward the door. I paid my check and followed. He didn't seem to want to talk yet, walked a step ahead of me all the way back to our building. The lobby was still open, but most of the offices were dark as the last sunlight topped the peaks of the San Gabriel Mountains to the east. When we left the elevator, I turned toward our office. Behind me, the big man stopped.

"This way."

He stood half-turned toward the other end of the corridor. Past him, Mildred waited far down near the fire door and the rear stairs. She hugged herself down there, as if cold.

"You're not Robert Peterson?"

"Shavitz, the building manager." He moved his head in the direction of Mildred and the far end of the corridor. "I think he's down there."

He was right.

He stood watching as I stepped back from the dead Robert Peterson. I held the dead man's hair in my hands. What had looked like his long blond hair. It was a wig. Under it his hair was still blond, but it wasn't long. It was shaved on the sides, a two-inch roach like a Mohawk in the center, and dyed with one blue and one red stripe.

"Call the police," I said.

TWO

Detective Two Rostov came from the Wilshire division. "Delaney was wrong, the guy's name was Robert Peterson all the way: driver's license, credit cards, voter registration, Blue Cross, auto insurance, library card, the works. M.E. says he's been dead since about four-thirty this afternoon. Knifed at close range. In under the rib cage and up. Twice at least. Blood all over the closet, none in the corridor, so he had to have been killed right in that closet. Walked along, forced inside, and killed. Quick, hard, and sure. No one heard anything or saw anything so far. Where's Delaney?"

He was a short, stocky, black-haired man in his mid-forties. He wore a neat two-piece brown suit from somewhere like Sears, a worn white shirt, and a plain brown tie. The police aren't overpaid in Los Angeles. They aren't overpaid anywhere. They don't produce anything you can eat, wear, or hang on the wall.

"Away on a case, Pete," Mildred said. "Paul's out from New York to cover the shop."

"Tell me about Peterson," Detective Pete Rostov said. "What did he want with a private?"

"Nothing to tell, Pete. He called for an appointment three days ago. He sounded young and nervous, maybe scared. The appointment had to be today, exactly at four."

"Shaw?"

"I flew in around noon, never met him or talked to him."

Rostov thought for a time. I waited. It's one of the fringe benefits of being a policeman: the power to make people wait. Outside the office, the lights of Hollywood and Los Angeles spread like sequins down to the distant and unseen ocean. Rostov finally shook his head.

"Almost looks like a gang killing, but that kid was no gangster. Nothing we found shows any kind of trouble, except maybe the hair."

"You mean because it's punk?" I said. "Maybe he was a punk rock musician."

"I mean because he wore a wig," Rostov said. "Over the roach and stripes he wore nice, normal hair to hide it all."

"A disguise to come to our office?" I said. "Maybe he knew he was being watched, followed?"

"Maybe," Rostov agreed. "Or maybe more permanent. You sure you don't know anything about why he wanted to hire you?"

"Nothing, Pete," Mildred said.

I said, "Whatever it was, he was probably killed so he couldn't tell us."

"Or his problem just caught up with him," Rostov said.

We all thought about the problem that had caught up with Robert Peterson. Another young man in Hollywood for fame and fortune, who'd found a more permanent failure than most?

A detective came in with a slender young woman in a black jump suit, heavy silver chains around her neck, and short, spiked hair dyed blue and orange. The detective was being careful, polite, but his heart wasn't in it.

"Mrs. Peterson, Pete. The dead guy's wife," the detective announced to Rostov. "Sandra Peterson. She was home when we got there. She don't know any reason for him to get killed."

Sandra Peterson shook her head. Her large eyes were heavy with eye shadow and shock. Paralyzed eyes, not even in the room. Unaware of the room, of where she was.

"No." She went on shaking her head. "No reason. No."

I said, "Do you know why he wanted to talk to a private detective, Mrs. Peterson?"

She looked at me. "Private detective?"

"You didn't know?" Rostov said.

She had a long face with high cheekbones. A classic face, except for the spiked and dyed hair. Without the hair she would have looked like any cool Hollywood career girl. Her eyes changed. Aware of the office, of where she was. Something had happened, something in what had been said.

"No," she said.

"Or what trouble he was in?" I said.

She shook her head. "Nothing. I don't know nothing. We never done nothing to nobody! Robbie never hurt no one!"

Rostov said, "What did he do for a living, Mrs. Peterson?"

"He works . . . he worked for a tax guy."

"Tax guy?"

"You know, a guy does people's taxes, tells 'em what to do to get off the hook."

"A tax consultant?" I said.

"Yeah, you got it."

Rostov stared at her. "Doing what?"

She bridled. "Working on people's taxes, what else? Robbie was a hell of a good accountant. You think because we're punkers we can't do nothing? I'm a legal secretary. We work at good jobs just like everyone else!"

"The wig," I said to Rostov. "In a straight job, he had to wear his hair neat and proper. The wig was for the job."

"You got it," Sandra Peterson said.

Rostov nodded to Sandra Peterson. "You got a wig for business too?"

"None of your damned business."

Belligerent and defensive.

"Maybe your punk friends got rough," Rostov said. "They're all crazy anyway. Maybe there was trouble in the punk scene."

"The on'y trouble we ever had was when we was straight! Punkers don't hurt nobody. All punkers want is out, *finis*."

"Out of what, Mrs. Peterson?" Rostov said.

"Out of your sick world," Sandra Peterson said.

"Your husband got out," Rostov said. "You're sure it was just my sick world he wanted out of? You sure it wasn't something else, and someone didn't want him out?"

She only glared at him.

"Okay, we'll go in and get a statement the hard way. Everything you and your husband did the last month, maybe the last year. Especially everything you did today, who saw you, the works. Let's go."

No matter how good a cop is, there's no way he can avoid prejudice against those who defy the system. Not and stay a cop. His job is to defend the system, the views of the majority. To believe that the way things are is the right way, the only way.

"Hassle!" Sandra Peterson said. "That's all you cops know how to do. Hassle the punks! Hassle the kids! Hassle everyone don't play it your way! Well, I didn't kill Robbie, and I don't know who did, so take me in, you'll get shit out of me!"

She began to cry. The tears streamed down her long face with its classic cheekbones. Sat and cried, the belligerence suddenly gone, only the misery left.

Rostov nodded to his men. Two of them helped her up. She was still crying as they walked her out.

"Stick around, Shaw," Rostov said.

I nodded. Rostov followed the others out. Mildred and I sat in silence in Delaney's empty office. Mildred got up, put on her sweater, picked up her handbag. She looked unhappy.

"Does it bother you to let it just drop, Paul?"

"We're a business."

"I suppose," she said. "See you tomorrow."

"Not too early."

Alone, I turned off the desk lamp, sat in the dark, and looked out at the vast sweep of lights that was Los Angeles. The vertical lights of the distant high rises. The horizontal lights of houses and city streets. The moving lights of the freeways that made all the other lights possible. The far-off darkness that was sea and sky.

The city of shiny dreams and wild goose chases, and it looked like I'd come out on a snipe hunt myself. Maureen was not going to be pleased. I dialed. It was only midnight in New York. She should be at home and up. She was.

"Just fine," she said. "No case and you're three thousand miles away."

"I'll be home tomorrow."

"I could shoot John Thayer! Maybe I'll just buy him out."

"Unless Dick has another case for me."

I could see her perched on the edge of the bed in our Central Park South penthouse. Her penthouse. A small woman, slim, her dark red hair worn long because that's how the movie magnates and fan clubs like it. Shadowed eyes, a low, throaty voice, and a temper.

"For Delaney, you go to the Coast in an hour! For me, not in a year! How many times have I asked you to come with me, but you were working? For John Thayer you jump, for me you don't even amble! You know I'm stuck in New York on the TV special."

"I'm not in the movie business, baby. I wasn't a good enough actor, so I'm a detective. I'm a good detective. I try to earn my money."

"Well, I suppose it pays our taxes."

With her income, it doesn't really do that. Love, I heard someone say once, is harmony even in discord. Some actor playing a Chinese monk on television. It probably came from Confucius or Lao Tze, but they don't rate script credit at NBC.

"I'll be home as soon as I can. Love me?"

"Enough to murder, Thayer. Make it sooner, darling."

It isn't good for the spirit or the flesh to sit alone in a darkened room imagining Maureen getting ready for bed in New York. I got my jacket and headed for our hotel. The

telephone stopped me. It rang all the way to the outer door.
I went back.

"Thayer, Shaw and Delaney."

"Mr. Shaw?" It was Sandra Peterson's voice. "I want
you to find Robbie's murderer."

It was her voice, but there was something odd, different.
The same, yet not the same.

"The police will do that, Mrs. Peterson."

"Perhaps not soon enough."

"Does that mean you know why he was killed?"

"It means I'm scared. It means I don't know what I
know."

"Where are you?"

"At home." She gave me the address.

I said, "Mrs. Peterson? What's your real name? Your
husband's real name?"

There was a silence. "I'll tell you when you get here."

I got my little Colt Agent, took it down to the company
car with me, hid it under the front seat. In Los Angeles a
private investigator is not supposed to have a gun. Then I
went to meet Sandra Peterson.

Maureen was going to hate it, but Dick Delaney had been
right about Peterson's name. Maybe we were pretty good
detectives.

THREE

SHATTERING ROCK MUSIC came to meet me. At the top of a long, twisting drive up a steep slope in the Hollywood Hills of North Hollywood. Violent music among the palms and hibiscus. From an old ramshackle three-story frame house turned into apartments that overlooked the juncture of the Ventura and Hollywood freeways far below.

Sandra Peterson opened the door, smiled as I puffed from the climb. It was a small smile.

"The smog," I said. "In New York we have clean air."

She tried to go along with the joke—"That's what they all say"—but her heart wasn't in it.

A small living room was furnished with mattresses, orange crates, and Salvation Army rejects. Through an open arch I saw a small bedroom with an unmade double bed. The small kitchen wasn't even a real room. A tiny apartment even by New York standards. Shabby, but with a view as sweeping as all of Southern California. I stood looking out the high windows. The darker shadow of the San Gabriels was to the east across the San Fernando Valley. The Hollywood Hills themselves lay below, a broad seam of empty black between the endless lights of Los Angeles to the right and the San Fernando Valley to the left.

"We paid for the view," Sandra Peterson said. "We liked to sit and look out. It gave us something special." She thought about the view and something special. "I guess I'll have to move now." We all mourn in our own way, and I learned long ago you can't rush someone who's mourning. She would return to me in her own time, her own way. "Sit down, Mr. Shaw. I hope you don't mind the music."

She wore the same black jump suit and silver chains. She was smoking now, and that difference I had heard in her voice on the telephone was still there. Tight and nervous, but something else, too.

"I don't much like the violence," I said.

She gestured with the cigarette. "Everything is so neat today, so empty, so wrong. All surface. Polite and cerebral. We need some violence to make us wake up, look around."

"You should have been around in the sixties."

"But I wasn't, Mr. Shaw. Maybe that's exactly why we need the punk scene. Rebels without even the memory of a cause."

"Then why rebel?"

"Most people just sit and play the same movie their parents call life around and around, again and again. Some people have to try to make the world something other than they found it when they came in."

And then I caught the difference. The street speech was gone, the bad grammar and worse pronunciation. An educated voice with educated thoughts. The right words in the right place.

"Who was it all for?" I said. "The dropout act? The street speech?"

She shrugged. "It's what the police expect from a punker. You always give the police what they expect or they get confused and that makes them mad."

"That's the only reason?"

"No, maybe not." She stubbed out the cigarette. I was getting too personal. "Would you like a drink?"

"Scotch or beer."

She brought two beers. Beck's. Everyone travels high these days, even if most of them don't know where they're going. Then, Sandra Peterson and her husband had had two jobs and I saw no signs of children. The beer was good. She sat down in a seedy armchair. I was on a narrow couch. Every now and then, as she talked, a car passed and the house shook on its steep hill.

"I'm twenty-six, Mr. Shaw. Older than Robbie . . . was. What I said about the punk was true. I grew up and saw a world I didn't want. I knew what I didn't want, but not what I did. I don't know what I want the world to be, but I know that today isn't it. I always loved rock music, so I found the punk scene out of protest."

"And Robbie?" I said. "Is that how you met? The punk world? He was there when you found it?"

"I was first. I'd been a punker for years when a girl I knew brought Robbie around some of the hangouts. We liked each other. He liked the music and the independence, but he didn't like the violent overtones. I don't think he'd have stayed if we hadn't fallen in love, gotten married. And if it hadn't been a scene where people he knew wouldn't notice him."

She slipped it out like that, offhand and casual. Drank her beer and looked at the windows where the night chill was blowing in colder and the drone of traffic was a steady undercurrent to the rock music.

"Why didn't he want to be noticed by people who knew him?"

"So he'd be left alone. To be private, have a new life." She drank. She searched in the pockets of her black jump suit, brought out a cigarette. She lit the cigarette. "As soon as I heard you were a private detective, and Robbie had been coming to see you, I knew it had to be the old trouble. He said it was over, but it wasn't."

I said, "Why not start with his real name?"

She breathed. Deep breaths. "His real name was Robert Asher. Mine was Sandra Bridger. But that doesn't have anything to do with it. My name." She looked again towards the windows and the lights of Los Angeles, and the Valley spread far and wide below. "We'd only been married a year, or we would have been next month. I didn't meet Robbie until after . . . after it all happened." She smoked, drank. "I'm afraid. Afraid of what I don't even really know. Afraid of what I might know. Afraid to talk to the police. Someone murdered Robbie! Why?''

She stubbed out the barely smoked cigarette.

"Before all what happened?" I said.

She lit another cigarette. "Two years ago Robbie was a student up at UC Santa Barbara. He was a senior and a math whiz. Too bright for his age and too young for his status. Beyond math and physics, he was a boy, an emotional baby." The tape ended on the stereo. We both listened to the silence. "He was in love with a girl, Norma Powell, who was part of an alienated group on campus. Intellectuals, top students, and troublemakers. Bright young intellectual revolutionaries."

She put a new tape into the stereo deck. Her eyes were distracted, her mind not on what her hands were doing. Her mind with Robert Asher up at UCSB. Yet she still needed the music, the violent sound of punk rock, as if without it she would be naked in the world. As if it was all she had left. Something she could count on, trust not to change.

In the shabby armchair she closed her eyes, leaned her head back. "Two years ago they were all kicked out. Something about stealing tests and selling them. They were arrogant and defiant, and at the same time afraid of their parents, so they dropped out and went off on a year-long spree. On drugs, in protest marches and demonstrations. Roamed all over—lived off the land, you could say. Petty robberies and burglaries, shop-lifting, con schemes. Gambled in Reno and Las Vegas. Stole cars and sold them. Everything and anything, a big lark." She finished her forgotten beer almost angrily, smoked. "Their families all reported them missing, had the police looking for them. In the end they holed up in a rooming house here in Santa Monica. Broke, the police after them, hyped up and defiant as ever, and that's when the real trouble happened."

"What real—?"

I stopped. Someone was out on the top-floor landing. The detective's sixth sense, or maybe just alertness and good hearing. Call it experience. Whatever, someone was out-side the door and moving around softly. I wished I had my little Colt, but I didn't, and I had to know who it was. I stepped to the door, opened it.

A man stood directly across the narrow landing at the door of the other apartment. A large man, tall and massive like a super-heavyweight wrestler. He carried a briefcase, looked over his shoulder at me without curiosity, only a smile. A polite smile, and turned to the other door again, rang the bell. He waited. A weight-lifter in a three-piece blue suit. His shoulders, chest, and belly strained seams; cloth never intended to contain anyone his size. Salesmen usually came smaller, and a lot softer. Whistled under his breath and looked at his watch. Finally shrugged to himself and walked away down the stairs without looking at me again.

A salesman with his briefcase. If anyone had opened the door of the front apartment, he would have tried to sell them something. I believed he would have. But he hadn't tried to sell me anything.

"Who was it?"

Her voice was scared. I closed the door.

"A salesman."

I returned to the couch, described the big man.

"I don't know anyone like that."

She sounded relieved but uneasy. As if everything was new to her, strange, almost unreal. I watched her as she sat there. She was a good-looking woman—girl—if it hadn't been for the spiked and dyed punk hair. Or was that my prejudice? Beauty is what we decide it should be.

"Tell me the real trouble," I said.

She listened to the heavy beat of her music. "They were holed up in the rooming house down in Santa Monica when someone came up with a scheme to make a lot of money. They were going to sell a big batch of illegal drugs, make a fortune. Not dope; prescription pills and capsules, the overproduction of some large pharmaceutical company. Seconal and Amytal and benzedrine and amphetamines.

Robbie never told me what company or how they got their hands on the pills. He never really told me what happened, just that they tried to sell the pills and the police caught them." She looked around the room as if she wanted to ask Robert Asher to tell her more now. Or just wanted Asher. "He didn't like to talk about it. It was something he'd done in another life, another world. When he was a stupid, over-educated kid."

"He was out on parole already?"

"On bail. The trial hasn't happened yet. The grand jury took over six months to indict them—I don't know why—and so far a firm date for the trial isn't even set. They're all out on bail. I don't know what happens now."

"Who are the other two? Besides Asher and Norma Powell?"

"Hal Brownlee and Eliot Drake."

"Where are they?"

"I wish I knew. When Robbie was released, he broke with them all, wanted to stay as far from them as possible. That's one reason he changed his name, bought the false identification."

"What was the other reason?"

"The job in the tax office. He was afraid they wouldn't hire him, and it was the best-paying job he could find. So he did a balancing act. He wanted to have enough money in the bank to help me out while he was in prison."

"He was so sure he'd go to prison?"

"He planned to plead guilty, Mr. Shaw."

"What did the others plan?"

She shrugged. It meant she didn't know, and it also meant she was pretty sure they didn't plan to plead guilty. They might not have liked what Asher planned. One guilty plea among four codefendants could ruin a whole defense.

"When did you get married?"

"After he got out on bail and took the Peterson name. He didn't want me to be Mrs. Asher." She picked up her ciga-rette, but it had gone out while she talked. She threw it away, lit another. "He'd really broken up with Norma before they were all caught. He'd wanted to leave, get away from them, even before the big scheme, but he didn't, and he paid. He was trying to make the break when we met. I suppose that's why he let Doreen bring him around. When it all finally blew up, he wanted me to leave him, but I wouldn't. So we got married and waited for the trial."

"Hiding out as punkers."

"There's nothing wrong with punkers!" It was her vulnerable point. Maybe because she was afraid there was something wrong with punkers after all. Something that had gotten Asher killed. "Punkers don't do any harm. We just want a different life from this nine-to-five, beer-and-bowling consumer society we have! We hate the commercialism, the greed, the indifference."

She stood up to get two more Beck's. She changed the tape again. All three tapes sounded the same to me. Everyone has his own way of getting through the world. Only Robert Asher hadn't made it very far through. Something in his world had killed him.

"You think it was the big deal that got him killed?" I asked when she returned with my beer.

"What else could it have been? What else could he have wanted to talk to you about?"

"You tell me."

She shook her head, almost tenderly. "He wouldn't have wanted to worry me. That police detective said he talked very low when he called your office, insisted his appointment had to be four P.M. today. That means he called from his office so I wouldn't hear. He made the appointment at four because today's my meditation class and I don't get home until almost six. It had to be something he was afraid I'd worry about if I knew."

Her beer was untouched this time. She hadn't lit another cigarette. Instead she looked again out her high window at the lights of the city and the Valley on both sides of the dark scar of hills, and the moving lights of the freeway.

"He'd been disturbed lately. Nervous. Even scared. I didn't know why, but it began when a series of articles about their case started in *Western Ways*."

"Why would a mass magazine be interested in four college kids and a small-time drug deal?"

She picked up her beer, drank. "Their families are important, all except Robbie's. Hal Brownlee's father is high up in some Hollywood studio, and that's always good copy out here. Eliot Drake's parents are right-wing money people from down on Balboa Bay—friends of Nixon, political. Norma Powell's family are landed old Santa Barbara socialites. Position, money, politics, and movies. Robbie was the one who didn't fit in. I guess that's why no one ever came to interview him for the articles."

"What do the articles say?"

"He didn't want me to read them," she said. "He clipped them out of the magazine and kept them, but he asked me not to read them." She shook her head. "I thought he'd come to terms, Mr. Shaw. He was resigned to paying for his mistake. I thought he was at peace with himself. Then the articles seemed to bring it all up again. He even started drinking, pacing around all night."

"Do you have the articles?"

She stood. "After I called you, I looked for them. I almost gave up. Then I found them hidden under the lining of his bottom bureau drawer. I didn't have time to read them."

"I'll read them. Pay me something. Whatever you can."

She wrote a check for three hundred, and I left her still listening to her violent music. Alone in the shabby chair in her black jump suit and silver chains under the dyed hair. Somehow the whole outfit didn't fit her voice or manner or what she had told me about Robert Asher.

FOUR

VOICES ECHOED UP from the pool below in a curve of the elegant hotel. I lay in bed in the sun and cool morning air of Southern California, trying not to think of having to call Maureen and tell her my case had come back to life, and with the memory of a brawny salesman who had not tried to sell me anything. I told myself Maureen would be at the TV studio, and called room service for breakfast.

Eggs and bacon out of the way, I sat with a pot of good hot black tea and read the *Western Ways* articles. There were five of them, each featured prominently in the bi-weekly over the last three months. The same author was listed on each: Don Mills, with no description of him other than "free-lance reporter and writer." Each article showed photographs of the four young criminals. I looked at the face of the living Robert Asher, a.k.a. Peterson, for some time. A slender boy, average from top to toe: nice face, soft eyes, a wispy mustache then, an eager smile. A mature man in math, an adolescent in love.

Then I read the articles.

When I put down the last issue of *Western Ways*, my tea had grown cold. I rang room service for another pot and took my shower. Showered and awake, with the fresh hot tea, I thought about what I had read.

In essence, the articles told the same story Sandra Peterson had: Four militant troublemakers at UCSB get expelled for stealing and selling examinations, go on a wild and violent spree over most of the western states, ending in a scheme to sell illegal pills that leads to their arrest. There were many more lurid details. Incidents to make the readers gasp. Titillations. But after I'd digested it all, the five articles didn't tell me much more than Sandra Peterson had.

But they told it with a very different slant.

The three men had been the planners, the schemers and movers, and Robert Asher had been the prime mover. The leader. The heavy. The constant implication throughout all five articles was that Robert Asher had been the whiz kid, the brilliant but twisted mind behind the baby face. He had all but kidnapped innocent young Norma Powell and forced her into a life of crime. The Svengali with hypnotic power over his trusting little sweetheart.

In the first articles the implication was subtle; only touched on, hinted at. Though it became stronger and more blatant later, it was never really obvious in any one piece. Only when the entire five articles were read one after the other did the slant become inescapable. Read over a period of almost three months, the bias would be hardly noticeable, but would build into a kind of subliminal brainwashing toward a single conclusion. A conclusion the opposite of the story Sandra Peterson had told. The story Robert Asher must have told her. And I could see why Robert Peterson-Asher had been disturbed by the articles. As the ringleader, the evil genius, Robert Asher would be in a lot more trouble with a jury. It would play hell with a guilty plea, make it look like nothing but a cynical attempt to throw the guilt on the "innocent kids."

I could see why Peterson-Asher would have wanted to hire us; to expose the articles if false, try to stop any more of them if true. I could even see a motive for Robert Asher to go out and kill a few people. But what was there in the articles to make someone kill Asher?

FIVE

THE OFFICES OF *Western Ways* were at 9220 Sunset Boulevard, just at the border where Sunset leaves the Strip and enters the peace and quiet greenery of Beverly Hills. I parked our company car under the building, took the elevator. It opened directly into a plush reception room.

The standard centerfold blond sat behind an orange and brown free-form desk that looked like a diseased kidney. The thick carpet was light brown with an abstract green cactus design. The walls were blue, with distant mesas and peaks. The whole effect was a gaudy desert sunrise, or maybe sunset, with a painted interstate highway that vanished straight ahead into an endless distance behind the kidney desk and the blond. It made me hot and tired.

"May I help you, sir?" Blond but not dumb. Smooth, clean, Stanford speech. The Western version of Vassar.

"I'd like to talk to one of your writers, if I may," I said in my best Eastern Seaboard diction. "A Mr. Don Mills?"

She briskly thumbed a Rolodex on her desk, and I watched her eyes change. Only a flicker, and then all smooth again as she picked up the interoffice phone and spoke low. When she hung up, her smile was in control.

"It seems that Mr. Mills is a free-lance writer, Mr...?"

"Paul Shaw."

"He doesn't work here, Mr. Shaw, but our editor, Mr. Engberg, would be glad to talk to you if that would help."

"I'll talk to almost anyone." I smiled.

Her smile froze just a little. Nobody really likes being mocked.

"If you'll take a seat, Mr. Engberg's secretary will be out."

She bent to the interoffice phone again. I sat on a leather chair in the shape of a saddle. The only cliché missing was a blowing tumbleweed and a mechanical bull. A new woman appeared.

"Mr. Shaw?"

The new one took me through a door painted to look like the gates of a corral under an arch emblazoned with the brand WW. An older woman who looked grateful for her job. The secretary of a man who tended to business, Mr. Murray Engberg, according to the lettering on his door, was vice president and editor-in-chief.

"Shaw, is it? You have a card?"

I gave him my card, watched him read it. A short, skinny man, maybe forty, with the beginning of a rich-food paunch. A softly draped five-hundred-dollar blue pinstripe suit that hung effortlessly from his narrow shoulders, and a complacent vest with gold watch chain and Phi Beta Kappa key. He lived well on his brains, Mr. Murray Engberg, and from the steel in his flat eyes as he read my card, he intended to keep it that way, had little interest in talking to a private detective.

"What do you want with Don Mills?"

"Some talk about the articles on the kid drug peddlers."

"A strong series. Great reader interest."

"I'd have said narrow and small-time. Four dumb kids on a juvenile spree who got caught the first time they tried an adult crime. Not very interesting to anyone except their parents."

"I'd say you don't read today's magazines."

"You'd be right," I admitted.

He leaned across the desk to instruct me on today's magazines. "Punk kids, sure, but bright and gifted and upper-class. The elite. Everyone likes to read about the young and bright and privileged falling in the mud. Especially if there's sex and violence. The readers get to go along on the thrills of the kinky joyride, and enjoy the fall of the uppity kids too. The game and the defeat both, all vicarious and safe.

We even have a duped girl seduced and led astray by a boy. Every girl wants to be seduced and led astray, every boy wants to dupe girls, seduce them all." He leaned back, smiled. "And, their families are prominent, more or less public figures, and we make them seem even bigger than they are. The public eats it up. We're a nation of voyeurs."

"Nice," I said.

He didn't like my attitude. "And they're powerful examples of what happens to overindulged kids. Undisciplined, no real values, no parental guidance. Self-indulgent and without backbone, they run wild and harm innocent people. The whole series shows the need for the old, basic family values. The need in this country for family and morality and strong father figures."

"You believe any of that?"

"I believe in selling magazines." He leaned back. "What's your interest in the pieces anyway, Shaw?"

"They came up in a case," I said. "I just want to ask Mills some questions."

"Such as?"

"Who he talked to. Where he found his facts. How he learned the details of what went on among those kids."

"He can't tell you any of that, Shaw. We protect our sources." His skinny fingers played with his Phi Beta Kappa key. "What's your case anyway? Who are you working for?"

"I can't tell you those things, Engberg."

He twirled the key. "Has someone suggested the articles aren't accurate?"

"Let's say I've heard another version."

"Then you've heard wrong! We stand completely behind the articles as written."

"All I want to know is where you got the facts, who Mills talked to."

Engberg stood. "Mills's sources are all primary and unimpeachable, and we intend to protect them."

His voice was firm enough, but there was something uncertain about his eyes. His mouth opened again as if to say more, then closed, hesitated. I walked to the door to let him make up his mind. He finally spoke behind me.

"It has to be one of those bums, the boys. Or the parents of one of them. Which one, Shaw?"

I looked back at him. "Why would it have to be one of them? Because they're the only ones who know your articles aren't so unimpeachable?"

"Because they're the only ones who would want to deny the truth of the articles! May I ask which one?"

"You can ask," I said.

I closed the door behind me. I didn't walk away down the carpeted hall. I listened. I heard the phone receiver picked up, the sound of buttons being pushed. Engberg's voice. No words, but the tone was clear. Low and urgent.

SIX

THE COOL OF the ocean met me where Sunset ends at Highway 1 in Pacific Palisades. I drove on up the coast to Malibu.

Duncan Stone was an old friend from my acting days in New York. Before Maureen, even before Vietnam. He hadn't made it as an actor either, had become a magazine writer, a specialist in investigative articles, and lived in one of the beach houses that stretch for miles on the ocean side of Highway 1, blocking both beach and sea from the underprivileged.

I parked in the short space behind his garage, rang at his gate. Dunc is a tall, thin, cadaverous man with too little hair on top of his long head and too much on the sides and back, like an old San Francisco poet from the fifties, or a late-nineteenth-century Bible Belt politician. I hadn't seen him in ten years.

"How's New York?" he said as he opened the gate.

"Still there," I said.

"I miss it," he admitted, "but not enough."

Inside the fence was a wooden deck where he sunbathed nude. Across the deck, sliding glass doors opened into the house that was essentially one large, bright room with glass walls that seemed to bring the great sweep of the ocean directly in. The house was so high you could see only water and space unless you stood at the very front and looked down at the beach below. The room all sea and sky, with a sense of flying and only Japan or infinity ahead.

"I guess it beats even Central Park as a view."

"Why don't you move out, Paul? Maureen could afford forty times this place."

"With change," I said. "She's a stage actress, Dunc; she belongs in the theater. Movies and TV are for money, the transient buck. Live out here, and sooner or later you stop going back."

"Depends on your susceptibility quotient and your cynicism rating," Stone said. "Drink?"

There was a long wet bar in the corner nearest the small kitchen. Comfortable chairs and couches were scattered around the big room. A free-standing metal fireplace dominated the center. Stairs to the right led down to the bedrooms.

"I'll take a beer."

Stone poured a bottle of New Albion ale from up in Napa. He pointed to a leather couch that faced the front glass and the sweep of the sea, slouched into an old purple sling chair I remembered from his last New York apartment. Wiry and all muscle in Levi jeans and a blue work shirt, he biked everywhere, did two hundred sit-ups each morning, and lived alone on his beach.

"You didn't come for a beer," he said.

"You do any any work for *Western Ways*?"

"Used to. They pay pretty well for a local rag. That's the way the magazine business is moving. It's easier to print now, and advertisers are putting their bucks into regionals."

"You don't work for them now?"

"Not with the current editor."

"Murray Engberg."

"You know him?"

"Since about an hour ago. I didn't like him either."

"What did you want with Engberg?"

I told him. He listened and sipped at his beer. He watched a solitary fishing boat out beyond the first line of breakers. I finished with my final debate with Murray Engberg. Stone leaned forward in the sling chair, something very like excitement on his lean face.

"Robert Asher's dead?"

"Yes. You knew him, Dunc?"

"Not exactly," he said. "Sandra Peterson—or Asher—told you there's something wrong with those articles in *Western Ways*?"

"She told the story differently, and she said the articles disturbed Asher, even scared him."

"Differently how?"

"Different details, different people. The same names, but not the same actions. According to Sandra Peterson, all four of the kids were in it equally, with Asher coming in last, brought by Norma Powell. That must have been what Asher told her. The *Western Ways* articles make Asher the leader, the other two boys right behind him, and Norma Powell dragged in by Asher."

Stone finished his ale, got up, held his hand out for my glass. I emptied it easily. It was beautiful ale. Stone returned with two full glasses, sat down again in the purple sling.

"You knew Robert Asher's name," I said. "You knew all their names and most of the story before I told you."

"It's my territory, Paul—that's why you came to me. You got a little luckier than you expected." He set his beer on a coffee table. "About a month ago I was approached by *Mother Jones*, *California Magazine*, and *People* to do pieces about those four kids and their spree. I'd been reading *Western Ways*, had done crime sagas before, so I agreed and went to work. Or I tried to go to work."

"Who stopped you? Engberg?"

"Everything stopped me. I'd never heard of Don Mills, tried to reach him through *Western Ways* just as you did. I got the same stone wall from Engberg. So I went to the writers' organizations. No Don Mills is listed as a member of any of them. That's damned unusual, but it was possible he was a newcomer who fell into the story somewhere out of town. It has happened. So I forgot about contacting Mills, and started to dig into the articles themselves."

"What did you get?"

"Confused," Stone said, drained his glass of ale. "When I tried to trace the people quoted, I found that specific locations were almost never given for anyone. States, areas, towns, but no neighborhoods, streets, companies, work places, anything specific. The more I looked, the more it was mush. Nothing I could pin down as sources, data, facts. I couldn't even find the three boys. They were out on bail, and no one could or would tell me where they were. I did locate a few minor people up in Santa Barbara: an Isla Vista landlord; a Goleta waiter; a university librarian; a few students. But after meeting them I wouldn't trust a word—I'm not sure they knew the four kids at all."

"You weren't able to trace or check anything?"

"In a nutshell," Stone said. "Except for one thing. I found Norma Powell."

"What did she tell you?"

"That the *Western Ways* articles are about the way it all happened, but she never talked to any Don Mills."

"Where is she now?"

"Up in Ventura. Living alone in a cottage, working as a cocktail waitress in a small nightclub, waiting for the trial."

"Give me the address, Dunc."

"No way." He grinned at me. "I'll lead you up there; you don't cut me out of this."

SEVEN

SOME SEVENTY MILES north of Los Angeles, Ventura sits on a flat coastal plain where two rivers come out to the sea—the Santa Clara to the east, the Ventura on the west—ringed by low foothills with mountains to the northwest. The houses climb up the slopes to the foothills, and the freeway cuts the town off from the sea.

Duncan Stone parked his old green MG at a small cottage on a street without a sidewalk and I drew up behind him. Weeds grew up along the road and behind the fences. Skinny stray dogs watched us warily from empty lots. The dry, dusty fields behind the houses sloped down to rocky little gullies not deep enough to be barrancas or even arroyos. The cottage itself had flaking white paint and green shutters, a bare front yard, and a rutted dirt driveway to a collapsed garage at the rear. Little more than a shack, but the windows were clean, the porch swept, and curtains were visible behind the clean windows. An old green Honda Civic stood in the driveway.

Stone knocked at the front door.

"Mr. Stone. Come in."

She was a small girl, large-eyed and soft-spoken. She gave Stone a smile but didn't even look at me, as if strange men had not been good news to her. She wore denim jeans and a T-shirt, her hair pulled back by a rubber band, a dust rag and spray can in her hands. Her size, the jeans, her soft voice and manner, made her seem younger than she probably was—somewhere around twenty-two or twenty-three. But her blond hair, full breasts, and curved hips made her look older. A shy face and a bold body.

"Have you found the boys, Mr. Stone?"

The tiny living room was clean and neat. The furniture was the anonymous kind you get in rented rooms, with nothing of her own added. Sparse and spartan. The bedroom through an opened door looked just as bare, and a doorless closet held no more than four or five items. It looked like a monk's cell, as if Norma Powell had withdrawn from the world.

"Not yet," Duncan Stone said. He glanced at me. He was asking if he should tell her about Robert Asher. I shook my head. He said to Norma Powell, "This is Paul Shaw. He's a private detective who wants to talk to you."

She looked at me for the first time, gave me a nervous smile.

"I'm glad to meet you, Mr. Shaw."

"Why are you living here, Miss Powell?" I asked. "Working as a waitress?"

"Instead of doing what?" she said. "Being where?"

"Being in Los Angeles or with your parents. I'm sure you could get a better-paying job in Los Angeles."

"Maybe I could," she said. She sat down on a sofa that raised a faint cloud of dust, motioned for us to sit. "I wanted to get as far from L.A. as possible. I'm not with my parents because I've caused them enough trouble. They need some time. Time for their friends and neighbors to forget me. I don't want them to go through all this waiting or through the trial. I'm working as a waitress so I can pay my own way, and in Ventura there isn't much else I can do. I don't type, take shorthand, operate a computer, or sell real estate."

"Then why live in Ventura?"

She half-smiled. "Because my parents live in Santa Barbara, close enough if I need them. I guess I'm not really as tough as I thought I was."

She sat looking down at the floor. Like someone beaten down by too much. Too much of everything.

I said, "Tell me about the articles in *Western Ways*?"

She shrugged. "I don't know why anyone would want to read them, but I guess they've got it sort of right, if that's what you mean. It was kind of strange to read about myself, remember all those things we did."

"What do the other three think about the articles? Did any of them talk to you?"

She shook her head. "I haven't seen them or talked to them since we were let out. I don't even know where they are."

"If that writer didn't talk to you, where did he get what he wrote?"

"I guess he talked to the boys, and all those people who knew us and what we were doing."

She sighed, just sat there with her hands in her lap, as if thinking of all the people who had known the four of them on their spree of defiance and rebellion and, in the end, crime.

"You're saying the articles are all true, Norma?"

She looked up. "You don't think they are?"

"I don't know what they are yet."

She shrugged again—the all-purpose gesture of so many young people. "They're mostly true, but I don't expect everyone's going to believe them. Maybe not anyone." Her voice grew bitter. "Oh, I know what people say about us, about me with three boys. Well, I'm going to pay for what I did even if none of it was my idea. I went along with it. I could have pulled out, even tried to stop them, but I let Robbie lead me on. I let Hal and Eliot and Robbie make me do what I didn't want to do, knew I shouldn't do. Oh, I was wild up in college. I liked driving the professors crazy. But I never wanted to do any of the stuff we did later. I know they won't believe me." She looked at both Stone and me. "You two don't, do you? The spoiled little elite girl and her kinky kicks at the expense of other people, right?"

Bitter and defiant, she said it all straight out, looked us and the world in the eye.

"The articles would make most people see your side, Norma," I said. "Even go easy at the trial."

She shook her head. "No, Mr. Shaw, everyone will say *Western Ways* just wants to sell magazines with a sensational story. We did it, and we'll pay. All four of us."

"Three of you," I said, watching her face. "Robert Asher was murdered yesterday in Los Angeles. On his way to my office to talk to my partner."

She was still looking straight at us, the finality of decision on her face, the immediate future settled, and something large and dark passed behind her eyes.

"Murder? Robbie? Why? Who? How?"

Each word clicked out like slides being changed on an automatic carousel. The click of word to word.

"You don't have any guesses about who and why?" I said.

Shock in her voice. "Who would want to kill Robbie?"

Shock and fear. She was stunned, and she was scared. I know real shock, real fear, when I see it. She didn't know who had killed Robert Asher, and she didn't know who could be next.

"You don't know anyone who could want Asher dead?" I said.

"Or any reason for killing him?" Stone asked.

"Reason? No, nothing." She shook her head, stared at us. "No one had a reason. No one would want to kill Robbie."

She went on staring at us and shaking her head in the tired little room of the rented cottage. Then she stopped moving. Stopped shaking her head. She seemed to listen to some distant voices out on the street. Voices speaking Spanish. The passing of some cars and a truck on the nearest main street.

She stood. "I'm sorry, I forgot. I have an appointment. I've got to get ready now."

I said, "Asher's wife thinks the articles disturbed him, maybe scared him. She thinks they were what he wanted to talk to a private detective about."

"I'm really sorry," Norma Powell said. "But I do have to get dressed. It's an important appointment."

I said, "We know Don Mills never talked to Asher, either. That leaves only the other two boys."

"I suppose so."

She turned and walked into the bedroom, closed the door. We didn't count anymore. We weren't even there. I nodded to Stone and we left. Outside at our cars, Stone looked back at the dilapidated cottage with its bare dirt yard, the ragged brown fields behind it.

"She was shocked," he said. "About Asher."

"She was scared," I said.

He nodded. "Because she doesn't know who killed Asher or why, and maybe the killer's after her, too."

"Because she does know who and why," I said. "She didn't know at first, but it came to her while she sat there. An idea anyway, a possibility. A strong possibility."

"What do we do?"

"You go back to Malibu, try to dig out this Don Mills, pin down those articles."

"And you?"

"I'll see what she does. Follow me, but no matter what I do, just keep going to the freeway. I'll call you later."

I drove away with Stone close behind. When we turned the first corner out of sight of the cottage, I pulled to the curb. Stone drove on past. I slumped down in the car where I could still see the cottage between houses, waited.

Less than fifteen minutes later the green Honda backed out of the driveway and headed for my corner, went past me, drove on toward the freeway. I gave her a block, then followed. A mile along she beat a red light and left me trapped. By the time I got through and reached the freeway she was nowhere in sight.

I took the freeway south. It was a fifty-fifty bet. I drove fast, passing cars, looking for the green Honda. When the Coast Highway split off at Oxnard, I hadn't found the Honda. Either she was driving even faster than I was, or she'd gone north. The only question was had it been luck, or had she wanted to lose me?

EIGHT

AT THE TOP of the steep curves of the Conejo Grade, the first stifling gusts of a Santa Ana blew through the flat expanse of the Conejo Valley and the San Fernando Valley beyond. The temperature jumped twenty degrees in a matter of minutes as I drove on through Thousand Oaks and Westlake Village. Sudden scouring bursts swept the freeway and threatened to push my car off the road with the blowing dust and leaves.

By the time I reached downtown Los Angeles and the courthouse, it had become a steady wind that bent the palms and blew the skirts of the women. The scorched breath of the desert. It was almost 5:00 P.M., and the assistant district attorney they gave me stood at his window and looked down at the streets. His attaché case was packed on his desk.

"The goddamn freeway is going to be an oven. Make it fast, Shaw, okay? I want to get the hell to the club and the pool. We've got a full-size Olympic pool right beside the bar, and on a Santa Ana night I need both."

"As fast as you can fill me in on the case."

"What do you want to know?"

"Everything you can tell me."

I sat down facing his desk. He stood as if he'd hoped I wouldn't really sit down, would change my mind and go away. He looked down at the streets again.

"Four losers from good families. Ingrates, troublemakers. Kicked out of the university when they had every damned advantage. Snot-nosed rebels off on a big ego trip of mayhem and just plain crime who ended up getting caught. I'm sorry for a lot of the people I prosecute, but those four aren't among them. They can rot in prison once

I've convicted them, and I will. They wanted out of their parents' world, and as far as I'm concerned they can stay out. They rejected the mainstream, the stable life, and they can take the consequences."

He looked at his watch.

"Fill me in on the actual crime."

He sighed, sat at his desk. I wasn't going to go away. "They tried to sell a truckload of prescription pills to various 'clinics' we know are nothing but drug fronts where wealthy users go for their fixes. We're always busting the 'clinics,' but they always start up again—new place, new name, new phony front, same owners. The trade's just too lucrative, the demand too constant, the risk too minimal. Small fines and wrist-slapping—and not even that with the lawyers they can buy. To get rid of them would mean changing the whole society, and we don't want to do that. But we can stop a lot of their drug suppliers, put on enough pressure to keep them from becoming too obvious or numerous. Those four kids were amateurs. A sweet arrest for the police, a piece of cake for me."

"You got the clinic they dealt with too?"

"It was clinics they tried to deal with, which was dumb in the first place. Yes, we closed the clinics involved, but they'll bounce back. Probably already have. The resilience of free enterprise."

"Where did college kids get a truckload of pills to sell?"

"No idea," he said. Lightly and easily. It wasn't his concern. "A lot of pharmaceutical companies make production overruns and sell the pills clandestinely to wholesalers who sell them to the pushers, but in this particular case I don't know the source yet, maybe never will, and I don't particularly care. Those kids had it all smooth and straight and they blew it. Who needs them, right?" He waited for some kind of applause, at least a nod of agreement. When he didn't get it, he shrugged. "The cops are still working on the source, one reason the trial's been delayed so long. None of those punk kids will talk, but it doesn't matter. I don't need the source to get them. We caught them redhanded; we've got the customers. Once I get going, the trial shouldn't last two days.''

"What else is holding it up? Besides the source?"

"Damned if I know. The preliminaries are taking forever, my boss says. All kinds of tactics by some of their lawyers. With four of them being tried together, the paperwork is fantastic. But I don't care how long it takes—I'll nail them cold.''

He was good and they were bad. He deserved his ease and his pool. He'd done everything he was supposed to. They were worse than bad. They had betrayed their privileged world, his world.

"What about those articles in *Western Ways*?"

"What about them?"

"Are they true? Was Robert Asher the leader?"

"You'll find that out at the trial."

"Is that what you told the writer Don Mills?"

"I never met any Don Mills."

"Where are they living now?"

"How do I know? They're out on bail. Their lawyers should know where they are. Supposedly they haven't left the county, but I wouldn't bank on it. As long as their lawyers can produce them, we don't worry too much about details. Maybe they'll jump bail. Then they get the whole book.''

"One of them won't jump bail, will he?"

He blinked at me. His pool and the Santa Ana were forgotten for a moment. "You know about Asher?"

"He was coming to see me when it happened."

"About what?"

"He never reached me. Have there been any new developments in the case you know about?"

"None, and Asher's death won't change a thing except now we've only got three. Anything else, the cops'll tell me.''

"You have the address of that rooming house in Santa Monica where they lived when they sold the drugs?"

He rummaged through his desk drawers, found a thick file, gave me the address in Santa Monica.

"If the writer of those articles didn't talk to you, where did he get the facts in his stories?"

"I have no idea, and I don't think I care." He looked at his watch once more. "Now I have to get home. The freeway will be a nightmare."

He picked up the attaché case and was gone before I could even stand. I sat there for a time while his secretary continued to type in the outer office. Then I lifted his telephone receiver to see if I'd get an outside dial tone without going through the secretary. I did. I dialed Duncan Stone in Malibu. The city of Los Angeles could afford it.

"Any luck?"

"None."

"No smell of Drake or Brownlee?"

"Not yet."

"You tried their lawyers?"

"First place I went, for Christ sake! How do you think I found Norma Powell? None of the other lawyers would give me anything. All hired by the families and not talking to anyone, especially the press, except Norma's shyster."

"Asher's lawyer, too?"

"He had a public defender. Asher only had a widowed mother somewhere up around Berkeley. The free mouthpiece wouldn't even see me."

I had the impression of Duncan Stone staring out in frustration at his private view of the ocean. The secretary stood in the open doorway with her handbag and an annoyed frown. I hung up and left.

NINE

A THICK HEAT had clamped down on the whole city, the hothouse air swirled by the gusting wind. On Ocean Avenue in Santa Monica I drove north along the high palisades above the darkening ocean, turned onto Wilshire, made a right on Twelfth Street, and then a left to the address where the four had holed up a year ago.

It was a three-story Victorian mansion with a neat sign hanging from a white pole on the lawn: *The Hartmann House for Actors*. It looked as if it belonged in some small midwestern town, but it was here among the palms and olive trees. No one answered my knocking. The half-glass door was open in the hot twilight.

Inside there was the cool stillness of polished bare wood in a wide entry hall. Stairs ahead, kitchen to the rear, and to the left a living room of overstuffed furniture, magazines, books, and a television set. To the right was a large dining room with a long table, around which stood perhaps twenty chairs. It reminded me of those New York and London boarding houses where actors lived at the turn of the century and on into the twenties before wars and movies and finally television wiped out a way of life.

"Are you an actor, young man?"

She came from the kitchen drying her hands on an apron. Short and plump in a print dress. Everyone's mother back in Iowa. But brisk, a certain raffishness about her. A cigarette in the corner of her mouth, the smoke closing her left eye. Rings on every finger, bracelets climbing her arms. Lipstick, mascara, eye shadow, and canvas track shoes. A crooked smile.

"You only rent to actors?"

"Not anymore, I'm sorry to say." She waved the cigarette smoke out of her eye and sighed. "They all own a house these days. In our time actors never thought of owning anything. Too much on the move, too busy working. Free and easy."

A short, stumpy old man with white hair and a cherubic face appeared behind the woman. "Businessmen and shopkeepers, that's all they are! The damned movies, then television, that's what ruined 'em." He wore a neat gray suit, blue-and-white bow tie, a jaunty flower in his lapel. Soft shoes that clicked as he walked. Tap shoes.

"Never owned a thing except our clothes and the trunk to put 'em in! The way it was since Shakespeare."

"Max and I played almost every city in this country and Europe, too," the old woman said, "before winter stock died and we came out here and went into the movies."

"Ruined us," Max snapped. "Ruined the profession."

"The silents weren't so bad, Max."

"Well, maybe not, but when the damned talkies started it was all over, Mabel, and you know it. Talkies and TV."

"Not all over, Max." The old woman, Mabel, smiled.

The old man winked at her. She slapped his rump. If I hadn't been there, I think they'd have taken their clothes off.

"You must be the Hartmanns?" I said.

"Mabel and Max," the old woman said. "When the parts ran out, we decided to open a boarding house like old-time actors did. We even had meals at first, but it all changed. Today it's hard to find actors who want to live in a boarding house. They all have cars, live on the beach or out in the Valley. We had to close the dining room." She brightened. "Still, we do get some young ones, especially when they first come to town."

"Can't even speak English." Max frowned. "There was a time you knew an actor as soon as he opened his mouth."

"Television audiences want actors to speak the way they do," Mabel said. "Bad grammar, terrible diction, uneducated accents, slurring speech, and the worst acting! Max did some commercials. He was fired for speaking too well, sounding too educated!''

I said, ''How did Norma Powell, Robert Asher, Eliot Drake, and Hal Brownlee come to live here? They weren't actors.''

''But they were,'' Mabel Hartmann said. ''At least, Norma and Eliot wanted to be. Eliot had real talent.'' She sighed again. ''I can't believe those children did what they say.''

''I can,'' Max snapped. ''That Drake was an arrogant pup.''

''A little self-centered,'' Mabel smiled, ''but Hal Brownlee was just a cut-up with no harm in him, and Robbie Asher was really quite a nice young man.''

''What about Norma Powell?''

''Tough cookie that,'' Max Hartmann said.

''She was always nice with us, Max,'' Mabel said.

''I said she was tough, not dumb,'' Max said.

I said, ''She was Asher's girlfriend?''

''We thought so at first,'' Mabel Hartmann said, ''but then she seemed jealous when Eliot Drake flirted with another girl in the house. Still, it's hard to tell just who is with whom today.''

''Asher started seeing that punker,'' Max said. ''Sandra something, remember? Brought her here a few times.''

''Did they have a lot of visitors?''

''Almost none,'' Mabel said.

''Have you heard from any of them since their arrest?''

''Not a one,'' Max said.

''How about forwarding addresses?''

''Just their lawyers,'' Mabel said. ''Except Norma Powell. She sent us a Ventura address a few months ago.''

''Adcock,'' Max said.

''Adcock, dear?'' Mabel said.

''George Adcock, second rear. Got that check from Brownlee. Should be an address on the envelope or the check.''

"I'd forgotten that." The old woman, Mabel, turned to me. "One of our tenants, Mr. Adcock, lent Hal Brownlee some money. A few months ago he got a check in the mail. From somewhere in Hermosa Beach, I think. Mr. Adcock's out now, but we'll ask if you can come back later or tomorrow."

I thanked the lively old couple and went back out to my car. It was dark now, the hot wind so thick in the night it was more like a liquid than a gas. I could feel the sweat under my shirt.

They were waiting at my car.

"Shaw?"

Both of them loomed large and expressionless in the night. They wore dark three-piece suits, white shirts, polite ties, and they weren't sweating. I was. One was the "salesman" with the briefcase who'd been on the landing outside Sandra Peterson's apartment. A long black limousine was parked behind my car. They took my arms, one on each side. I got into the limousine. It was air-conditioned.

TEN

WE DIDN'T GO far. Still in Santa Monica, we stopped in front of what looked like an English country pub. Half timbers, leaded windows, fake-thatch overhang on the roof, geraniums in flower boxes. The Wilshire Pub.

"Out and in."

The bar was crowded and noisy. An English-style bar with tall pump handles, the Watney red barrel on one, the Bass triangle on another. A blackboard announced other beers and ales from Britain and more distant lands.

"Over here."

Bare wood tables stood in the large room, and to the far left three dartboards with blackboards and rubber mats marked by white lines. One player stood practicing at the dartboards. Tall and gray-haired in a gray tropical suit with a blue-striped shirt and blue tie. Tropical suits usually look like wrinkled paper. This one hung so beautifully on the tall man it could have been cashmere. Under the thick gray hair, he had the craggy face of a middle-aged leading man with a cordovan tan that only comes from doing business by the pool in Palm Springs or conferring with presidents on a beach in Barbados. If the presidents were lucky. He looked maybe fifty, but from his neck, the liver spots under the tan, I guessed him at well past sixty.

"Damn!"

He flicked his darts pure English-style, all in the wrist and fingers and eye, and took the game seriously even when practicing alone. He turned to look at me as one of the big men retrieved his darts from the board. He had the cool blue eyes of a man who took almost everything seriously.

"You play darts, Mr. Shaw?"

"I've played."

He nodded to one of my escorts. I was handed three darts. Not pub darts, but good English darts he carried with him.

"What do you drink?"

I looked at the blackboard. "Taddy porter."

"Two Samuel Smith porters," he said to the big man. "You know English beer, Mr. Shaw."

"Do you want to tell me what—"

"I'll talk, Mr. Shaw. Shoot for start."

I shot a dart close to the bull's-eye. He shot closer.

"Learned during the war, acquired a taste for English beer." He missed the double twenty with all three darts. "They fly me a few kegs every month; I can never resist a dartboard."

I tried for the double six (the right side of the board is my side), missed with all three. One big man retrieved our darts while the other scored at the blackboard.

"I'm a strong admirer of your wife's work, Mr. Shaw, have even invested in her from time to time. A shame to spend so much time away from such a woman."

He missed the double twenty again all three times, muttered to himself. His concentration was off.

"A man has his work," I said. "What do you do, Mr...?"

"Shoot, Mr. Shaw."

I made the double six on my first shot, added 24 on the next two for 36 away. The muscleman at the blackboard scored me: 265.

"A woman like Maureen Shaw," the man in gray said. "A penthouse on the park. New York in the fall." He hit the double twenty on his second dart, said, "Yes," and shot his last dart into the single twenty: 241. "What more could a man want?"

"You didn't bring me here to discuss my happy home life," I said, aimed for the triple twenty. "What do you want, Mr...?"

"Don't question me, Shaw. I find it irritating. You were brought here because I have an important task I want done at once. Both your partners are busy, but I'm ready to pay a reasonable bonus for immediate action. Say, one hundred percent above your normal fee and expenses."

I hit the twenty twice, and a three: 222. "What task?"

"My people in London have the details. There's a red-eye from LAX that catches the early morning to London from Kennedy."

He hit two double twenties and a nine: 152. I missed the board with two darts, plunked the third in triple twenty: 162.

"Triple your fee and expenses," he said, "for an immediate departure to London. Mr. Delaney, too, when he is free."

He slipped two darts into the triple twenty, put the third into the double sixteen: 0 "Shot. You owe me a beer, Mr. Shaw. Two Taddy porters, Gabe. What do you say, Mr. Shaw? Yes or no."

"I say it's a pretty lame ruse to get me off the case I'm working on."

"Start," he said.

I missed my double six with all three. He hit his double twenty on his first dart, added 40 for 80 away and 221.

"Pretty lame," he said, "but I had no time to set up anything better. All right, let's talk about a straight bribe. Name your price to return to New York and forget four kids."

"What are those four kids to you?" I missed the double six three more times.

"Twenty-five thousand. No questions, no explanations."

He hit a triple twenty, a five, missed the double fifteen by the width of the wire.

"Is that twenty-five thousand each? Me and Delaney?"

"Is that your price?"

My second dart got the double six at last. I added a wild one for 288 to his 30.

"What's worth that much for me to not find it?"

"Is fifty thousand your price, Mr. Shaw?"

His voice was testy for the first time.

"Not fifty million," I said. "I don't like bribes. If I wanted money that much, I'd be in another business."

He hit the double fifteen with his first dart. "Shot. You could be badly hurt, Shaw. What's worth it?"

"What's worth so much to you?"

I shot again to start with a double six. I'm stubborn. This time I hit with my second dart, added 20, off at 269.

"Even your wife could be hurt," he said. "I'd hate to see anything happen to such a beautiful, talented lady."

He picked up double twenty with his first dart again.

I said, "You must be new at this. A lame con, a heavy-handed bribe, and threats that are sure to get my back up. And if you or either of those apes lay a finger on my wife, I'll kill you personally."

I missed the board with all three darts.

"No, you won't, Shaw." He hit three single twenties. I had a chance. "You would be dead long before you ever reached me."

"The way Robert Asher is dead?" I said, hit with all three darts for 68 and 201. Even.

The big man at the blackboard didn't score it. The other one, Gabe, didn't retrieve my darts. The man in gray didn't throw his next turn.

"Asher?" he said.

"Murdered. By a professional, probably. Maybe two professionals."

He handed his darts to the one doing the scoring. "You finish, Harry."

He walked toward the rest rooms at the rear. Gabe went to the bar. Harry shot the darts, hit two ones and a five. This one I could beat. I shot 54, took the lead at 147. Harry shot again, but I didn't see what he scored. Gabe was gone from the bar. I walked back to the men's room. It was empty. I went back to the dartboard. Harry was gone. Outside in the night the limousine was gone.

ELEVEN

I WALKED THROUGH the gusts of heat, falling palm fronds, dust-blown leaves to the Hartmann House. My car was still parked in front. There was light upstairs and in the hall. No one answered my rings. I went in anyway.

An old man sat alone in the living room, watching TV with the sound turned off. A baseball game. Dodgers against Giants up in Candlestick Park.

He spoke without looking at me. "Talk, talk, talk. You can't watch the damned game."

"Are the Hartmanns around?"

"Haven't seen them. Maybe back in their apartment. All the way back next to the kitchen."

I thanked him.

"Best rooms in the place," he said. "Not that the house ain't nice all around. Lived here twenty years. My son wanted me to live with him. No way. I know that game. Start telling you what to do, grab your money and send you off to some nursing home if you don't do what they want. I know the game. I . . ."

I left him watching the silent game, talking aloud to the empty room.

The apartment of Max and Mabel Hartmann had a fancy brass name plate and a polished brass knocker. No one answered the knocker, but the door was ajar. A dim living room was lighted only by a street lamp out at the curb. All the walls were covered with glassed picture frames that reflected the weak light from the street. It was hot in the dim room, but cooler than outside. The old house had been built when they still insulated houses in L.A.

I became aware of a shadow in a high-backed wing chair.

"Mrs. Hartmann?"

"They're not home."

I found a lamp.

The woman in the Queen Anne chair was small and compact, with very short blond hair parted on the side, mannish. She sat almost rigid in the chair. She looked at the walls of framed photographs, yellowed newspaper clippings, programs from theaters in most of the cities of the nation and Europe. The old couple in a hundred theatrical moments on a hundred stages. Forever young and forever eager. Middle-aged and intense. Old on soap operas even I recognized. Many of the pictures were with the famous, who would probably be surprised to know the old couple were still alive if they remembered them at all. Memory rests lightly on the rich and famous.

"They loved it," the woman said. "All those years."

Her voice was tired, as if she herself had gone through all those years on endless stages in endless cities before the empty eyes and slack mouths of endless audiences.

"Probably not enough years for them," I said.

"No," a tone of wonder in her voice, "they'd do it all again tomorrow."

She wore a narrow black pantsuit with a top cut like a dinner jacket, white blouse and jabot. As mannish as her hair, but there was no mistaking her for a man. Curved and full-breasted. A pale oval face with something regal about it. Large, magnetic eyes, and a thin, ascetic nose. No way to tell her age. Someone who took care of her appearance, was concerned with her appearance.

"Paul Shaw," I introduced myself. "When will they be back?"

"J.C. Connors. Probably soon. They go to bed early."

"You're looking for a room, Miss Connors?"

She turned her intense eyes toward me. "For a daughter, Mr. Shaw. She lived here once."

"Her name wouldn't be Norma Powell?"

"No."

She reached into a large black handbag and brought out a black-enamel-and-gold cigarette case. She lit her cigarette with a matching lighter. I hadn't seen a cigarette case in years. They had gone out after World War II with so many other upper-class customs.

"How long has your daughter been missing?"

"I haven't heard from Doreen in over a year." She smoked as the hot wind gusted outside and the old man talked to himself in the distant living room. "You're interested in Norma Powell?"

"You know her?"

"Doreen mentioned the name in a letter once."

"When?"

"About a year ago." She smoked. "In her last letter."

"What did she say about Norma Powell?"

"Just that she'd met her."

"In this house?"

"I suppose so."

"Did she mention Robert Asher? Hal Brownlee? Eliot Drake?"

"Who are they?"

I told her who they were. Her slim fingers turned the cigarette around and around, drummed on the arm of the Queen Anne chair. I finished with the *Western Ways* articles.

"Did you read them?" I asked.

"No. All out on bail?"

"It's taking a long time to get the trial started."

She stubbed out her cigarette, lit another. The sleek case was real gold and Chinese lacquer. An expensive case. She didn't look or act rich, yet she seemed somehow privileged. "Where are they now? Those four kids?"

"I only know where two of them are. Norma Powell's up in Ventura, and Robert Asher's dead."

"How did he die?"

"Murdered. By someone who had experience with a knife. Are you sure your daughter didn't know the boys, too?"

"No, I'm not sure," she said. "I'm not sure of anyone Doreen knew out here."

Before I could ask her where she and Doreen were from that made California "out here," there was an insistent knocking on the apartment door. A dapper old man as small and thin as a feather stood in the doorway.

"Who the devil are you?"

In a jaunty blue blazer, gray ascot, and gray slacks over white bucks, he barely came up to my shoulder.

"The Hartmanns are out," I said.

"Out? Ridiculous! Never out at night."

"I'm afraid this time they are."

"Sure, are you?" He peered up at me speculatively. "Selfish of them, I must say. Must talk to them, don't you know?"

"Come in then, wait with the rest of us."

He stepped back. "No, best not. Keep our privacy, eh? Ridiculous, out at this hour."

He marched away into the front hall. I went back to talk some more to J.C. Connors. The Queen Anne chair was empty. I listened but heard no sound in the apartment. Only the wind shaking the windows. I checked the bedroom, and the small kitchen. The back door into the yard was open, blowing. I waited another hour. Then I gave up. No sense being a damn fool. I left a note for the Hartmanns on an old envelope and went out to my car. There is never a time when the freeways are deserted, it would take me a good forty minutes to reach North Hollywood.

TWELVE

OFF THE FREEWAY the palms bent and whipped in the hot wind. It's always a shock, the hot surge of a Santa Ana against your face. Wind is supposed to be cool, to bring relief in the hot night. But when the Santa Anas blow down the canyons, the wind is hotter than the air inside a house. Unless on a night in September a hurricane sits down off Baja. Then a thick, oppressive heat lies over the city, and even the moving air of a Santa Ana is cooler.

It was a night like that as I turned up the twisting roads of North Hollywood toward Sandra Peterson's apartment.

It is hard to breathe on such a night, hard to move. The cars on the freeways seem weary. In the houses, long-married couples hate in silence. Newlyweds and lovers breathe slowly in the thick dark, think violent thoughts. Solitary people stare at the walls of empty rooms. Everyone knows they will never move again. There is no reason to move. The weight of infinity presses down.

The headlights flashed on.

On a hairpin curve. Lights and tires and engine coming at me. If I braked, the car had me, broadside and over the edge. I accelerated. It slid past behind me. Careened and vanished. Raked sparks from the guardrail as if exploding the thick night, and gone down a side road among the dark, silent houses.

Only the sound of air-conditioners in the heavy dark. And my breathing. Stopped, I held to the wheel, breathed.

After a time I became aware of the hot wind again, the heat of the narrow canyons on the silent streets that curved up the dark slopes. I started and continued on up. The houses were set back, lights feeble through hedges and trees, the few street lamps scattered. I drove and watched. It could have been an accident, a drunk or stupid driver, but I didn't think so. Somebody had wanted to kill me, or at least strongly discourage me, and would probably try again.

Almost at the top. It came without lights this time. From a darkened cul-de-sac. Invisible if I hadn't been waiting. A movement in the night to the left. Sudden engine, tire screech, and on me. Ready this time for my surge ahead, I jammed on the brake, slowed and skidded sideways. In front, it took my right fender. Passed screeching. Tried to make the turn down the hill, didn't make it. The guardrail was high here, and the car went under the rail to hang tilted over the edge of the drop. Hung swaying up and down, up and down.

I parked, took my little Colt from under my seat, walked to the car, its front wheels still spinning over the dark drop. There was no sound, no movement beyond the gentle rise and fall of the car, the spinning wheels. A fine new Mercedes. Without a top. Sheared off by the guardrail that still held the rear. Blood gushed across the hood, the real leather. Blood on me, over me. The body in the front seat had no head. A headless corpse in a three-piece suit with a Phi Beta Kappa key on the watch chain across the vest. I went back to my fenderless car, drove on up to Sandra Peterson's apartment.

She stared at me. At the blood wet on my hands, dark on my shirt and suit. A woman with long dark hair, beautiful.

"Sandra?" I said.

"The punk hair's a wig," she said. "What—"

"For your office work," I said. "Robbie wore a wig over punk hair; you wear a punk wig over real hair." I felt myself nod as if I had solved a great problem. "Where's the phone?"

She pointed. I called the police. I told them what and where and how. Then I called Rostov at Wilshire division. When I hung up, she was still in the open doorway.

"Murray Engberg," I said. "Editor of *Western Ways*. He tried to run me off the road, missed, hit a guardrail. A high rail. It took his head off. I'll be back."

I left my Colt, drove back down. It wasn't far. Rostov got there right behind the traffic patrol and the North Hollywood detectives. It saved me telling it all twice. They all listened, made their notes. The North Hollywood division and the traffic people did their work with the ambulance and tow truck and skid-mark measurements and angles and photographs. Rostov watched with me.

"He was out to kill you?"

"At least take me out of the picture."

"Because of those articles?"

"It's all I asked him about."

"Peterson, or Asher, is in the articles? The whole four of those kids?"

I nodded. They were taking the headless corpse of Murray Engberg out of the car. Something had been worth protecting, important enough to kill me to hide. Not important enough to die for, but desperate amateurs don't think of that.

"Something's wrong about those articles," I said. "It's all that makes sense. Engberg knew it. Got paid to forget what he knew. Maybe to print the articles in the first place. He was afraid I'd find out. He'd lose his job. Maybe worse."

"Tell me the rest so far," Rostov said.

I told him about Duncan Stone, and Norma Powell in Ventura, and the nameless dart player in the gray suit with his neat and well-dressed musclemen, and Murray Engberg. He wrote it all down, gave it to the North Hollywood detectives. They would be in touch with me later.

It was midnight before I knocked on Sandra Peterson's door again. She was still in her real dark hair and a slim sheath dress with only her slender body under it in the heat. A hard young body I saw now. Tight and tense. A pale blue dress. A small woman, barefoot, her eyes bright. Scared but alive.

"Are you all right?" She looked at the blood, now dry on my hands, dark on my suit.

"He wanted to hide those articles," I said. "There's got to be something wrong about them."

"You think that's what Robbie was going to tell your partner? Hire you to prove?"

"Maybe." I looked at the blood on my hands, my suit. "You have a shower?"

"In the bedroom. I'll get towels."

When she came back with the towels, the shaking had started. I sat on the small double bed. She watched me. I needed the shower, but if I tried to undress, my hands were going to shake like those of a drunk in Bellevue. She came and took off my jacket.

"You know a tall, good-looking, gray-haired man who looks and acts under fifty but has to be way over sixty? Rides around in a limousine with two large bodyguards, assistants, whatever?"

She unbuttoned my shirt, took off my shoes.

"He sounds rich. I don't know anyone rich. Robbie never knew anyone rich except maybe in college."

She'd undressed a man before. She pulled off the pants, dropped them into a pile with the jacket and shirt.

"How about Doreen Connors?"

"Doreen was the girl who brought Robbie around the punk scene. She was how I met Robbie, lived in the same rooming house with him."

I took my own shorts off.

"You don't know where they got those pills to sell?"

"No."

The shower was hard and hot, and I let it run long and slow until the shaking was gone. I could see her shadow through the steamed glass where she sat on the toilet seat.

"And you don't know our rich dart player?"

"No."

"He knows you," I said, "or at least Robbie. One of his goons was the man out on the landing acting like a salesman."

She opened the glass and began to wash my back.

"You've told me all you know, Sandra?" I said. "You were at that rooming house with Robbie back then."

"Only a couple of times. I never met the other three for more than a fast hello. I don't know who that rich man is or what he wants."

She washed me all over. I let her wash me. Perhaps it was the blood, the violence of a headless corpse in the hot night. She dried me all over. I let her dry me. We sat for some time on the edge of the tub while she rubbed me softly with the towel. Then she undressed, and I carried her to the big double bed.

She was small, slender, and smelled of soap, and the bed was close enough. Perhaps desire and fear are somehow the same. Hard thighs and tight buttocks. Open. Small young buttocks. Wide and hot and dark in the night. Sex and death. The violence and the inevitability. We needed each other in the big bed in the shabby apartment. Against the blood and absurdity, an indifferent world.

THIRTEEN

SHE WAS GONE in the morning.

I had a wife, and Sandra Peterson could be a liar or worse, but we had needed last night. Just needed, and you can't live apologizing for your needs.

She'd left some of Asher's clothes out. I found enough to cover me that more or less fit, put mine in a brown paper bag, drove back to our hotel through morning heat that was already in the nineties. When I got to the room, I sent my clothes to valet service, dressed in my lightest suit, a tan tropical, called our garage to pick up my battered car and leave a second, and went down for breakfast in the hotel dining room.

It was expensive—Thayer would disapprove—but it was too hot to walk the streets. The coffee was made by a chef and tasted the way coffee is supposed to taste, not like the gray-brown liquid they serve in plastic and cardboard coast to coast.

In the office Mildred had no news of Delaney. No one had called me. Not even Maureen.

I drove to the offices of *Western Ways* on Sunset. The centerfold blond behind the orange and brown free-form desk had dark circles around her eyes and a red nose as if she'd been crying all night. She tried to smile and failed, looked up at me as if she had some vague idea she'd seen me before. I asked for the publisher, or whoever the big boss was.

"Do you have an appointment, Mr...?"

"Shaw," I said. "No appointment, but he'll see me."

She tried to place the name, failed, and shook her head.

"I'm sorry, Mr. Forbes can't see anyone without an appointment this morning. We've had a terrible—"

"I know," I said. "I'm the man who came to talk to Engberg about Don Mills. The one he tried to kill last night."

The feeble smile she'd managed vanished. She swallowed, stared at me, licked her lips, and spoke low and fast into her mouthpiece. I waited on the thick carpet with its abstract green cactus design. The gaudy desert sunrise, or maybe sunset, hung over the distant mesas and peaks. A tall, stooped man in a soft charcoal-gray flannel suit, his hands clasped in front of him like a church deacon, seemed to come out of the painted interstate highway that vanished straight ahead into an endless painted distance.

"Mr. Shaw?" A quiet, firm voice like that of a church deacon.

"Mr. Forbes?"

"Dugald Forbes. The publisher. You wish to see me?"

"I wish," I said.

"Yes." He was not amused. "Come into my office, please."

I followed him through the door in the painted interstate and down the same corridor I'd entered by another route when I'd come to talk to Engberg. He took me to the far end and a large corner office with a much better view of the high rises jutting up out of the haze all across the vast sweep of Los Angeles. A view Engberg would never have, from the corner office that would never come.

"Sit down, Mr . . . Shaw."

I saw file copies of the magazines spread all across his desk. Five issues. I didn't have to think hard to guess which five issues they were.

"How do they check out?" I said, sat in a chrome-and-leather armchair facing him. It was an original Mies chair, the leather like soft chocolate cream.

He sat down behind the desk. "The police were here all morning, Mr. Shaw." He stared at the door as if still unable to believe that the police had actually been there. In his office. "I could tell them nothing. What can I possibly tell you?"

"Why Engberg tried to kill me."

"I have no idea why Murray would want to kill anyone."

"I do."

"Yes," he nodded. "The police suggested that you thought Murray could have wanted to kill you because you were asking about the articles of the juvenile crime escapades of those four poor dropouts. That is not possible. Those articles are—"

"I came to see Engberg yesterday about those articles. He wouldn't tell me anything. It was all I talked to him about. It was the only time I ever met him. He died trying to kill me."

"Yes." He nodded. "The police said that was a possible factor in his accident. But there has to be some mistake, some other explanation. It must have simply appeared as if he were trying to murder you, but that wasn't what he was doing at all."

I said, "It isn't *possible* Engberg was trying to kill me; it's certain. I don't *think* the articles were the reason; I *know* they were the reason."

He smiled, spread his hands almost in benediction. "But, Mr. Shaw, there is nothing at all unusual or even special about those articles. Quite routine, I assure you."

"Then why are you studying them?"

The smile remained, beatific. "But I'm not. I simply had not read them. I now have, and I have enjoyed them. Excellent work, a fine moral lesson for the young."

"If they're true."

"Our lawyers are quite calm."

"Which has nothing to do with the truth."

"A cynical view, Mr. Shaw."

"I'll give you another. You don't care if they're true or not, if ten more people are murdered or not. You'll protect the magazine. Murder, stopping more murder, stopping a criminal, doesn't matter as long as the magazine is safe.''

The benevolence faded only a little. ''Is there anything else, Mr. Shaw?''

''Has anyone else been asking about those articles?''

''Not recently.''

''But at some time?''

He considered. ''Some months ago our popular-music editor had a friend who asked about them. He happened to mention it to me. The lady never asked again, seemed to be simply curious about the four dropouts.''

''A lady? She have a name?''

''A rather well-known name, I understand: J.C. Connors. Some kind of entertainer. Not my field of interest.''

The lady in the dark at the Hartmann's rooming house. A lady just looking for a daughter who hadn't written in a while.

''How about a gray-haired man who rides in a limousine, plays darts, has two large 'assistants,' and seems to be interested in the four kids in those articles? A rich man, I'd say.''

''He sounds fascinating but means nothing to me.''

''I wonder if he did to Engberg? Or Don Mills?''

''I suggest you ask Don Mills.''

''Fine. Where do I find him?''

He spread those soft, unctuous hands again. ''Alas, I have no idea. Murray always protected his writers. He seems to have taken the information to the grave with him.''

''How will you get the rest of the articles?''

''Fortunately, they are all in-house now.'' He smiled. ''And Mr. Mills has been paid in full. We may never need him again.''

''I'd make book on it,'' I said. ''I wonder if Engberg's bank account suddenly got fat recently? The police will check.''

He nodded, grave now in his black. ''It seems Murray did have a new bank account, rather large, but it appears to have been an inheritance. Should it prove otherwise, we shall be quite shocked, I assure you.''

"And won't have any idea where it could have come from.''

He smiled. "None.''

"I hope it stays that way," I said, stood up. I smiled too. "If I ever prove those articles are fakes, and you knew it even after Engberg was dead, you'll be an accessory. If you knew before he was dead..." I let it hang there.

He stopped smiling and didn't look very benevolent. The deacon hands remained clasped in supplication as he stood with me, but the eyes had something other than a blessing in them. I walked to the door. It opened before I reached it. A short, dark woman with a pretty face and heavy, shapeless figure came in. Her face was a mess. Red and puffed and blotched. Forbes stepped around his desk.

"Ingrid? What do you...?''

The woman didn't look at Forbes, only at me. She came up to me, began to pound on my chest with slow, hammer-like blows of both hands. Began to cry. Hitting and crying.

"You killed him. He's dead...dead. What do I do now? You killed Murray!'' Her voice rose to a scream, faded. "What do I do now? She'll get it all. Everything. His fucking wife! You killed him!'' The scream again, and still pounding at me, pounding. "Nothing. I get nothing. He's dead. Murray! You killed—''

Forbes reached her, pulled her away from me. "Ingrid, stop it! If you don't stop, I'll have to—''

She turned on him, scorn and rage. "Get your fucking hands off me, you son of a bitch! What do I care what you do? Fuck your job! What do I care now? He's dead! Dead!''

Her voice shrill in the screams again. I left.

Down in the lobby, I waited where I could watch the stairs and elevators. She came out within ten minutes. Ingrid whatever-else-her-name-was. Her eyes were still red but dull now. I fell in step with her in the oven of the street.

"I didn't kill him, Ingrid," I said. "You know that."

For a moment I thought she would start screaming again as she looked at me. Then she turned away, watched the street.

"The rest of the day off to calm yourself?" I said.

"Forbes is all heart."

"Coffee? A beer? Iced tea?"

She stopped, looked up at me. "Look at me. Tell me where I find another man like Murray?" She turned slowly so I could see her thick body, her heavy legs, her poor clothes. "All you want from me is answers. I don't have any. I don't work in editorial, and Murray never talked business. All I can tell you is he was proud of the articles about those snot-nosed rich kids, said they'd boost circulation, maybe even win him a prize. Now let me go home and cry some more."

She walked away, steady and erect. I hoped she'd find someone a lot better than Murray Engberg.

FOURTEEN

THE REAL MEANING of a city that is built around the automobile can't be understood until you live in it. Everything is at least an hour's drive away. The Hollywood Freeway took me to the Santa Monica Freeway, to the Coast Highway, and up to Malibu.

Duncan Stone's old green MG two-seater was parked behind his beachfront house. He heard me, led me into the wide living room that seemed part of the sea and sky beyond its glass. We had coffee. The hotel made better coffee, but Stone had the view.

"Anything?"

He shook his head. "It feels like I'm going backwards. No one knows Don Mills. I'm beginning to wonder if he exists at all." He drank his coffee. "I haven't gotten near anyone named in the articles who'll talk to me. They could have been paid by *Western Ways* to keep quiet, or there could be something they don't want to talk about."

The hot wind seemed to ooze through cracks in the walls. I told him about the Hartmanns in Santa Monica, the rich dart player, and Murray Engberg headless in the hot night.

"Christ." He got up and walked to his wall of glass above the beach, watched the roll of the surf and the distant horizon over the vast sea. "What did he want?"

"He wanted to kill me," I said. "Stop me asking questions, rocking the boat, exposing something."

Stone didn't seem to hear me. "Sometimes, after a TV show or a movie about England in the old days, Henry the Eighth, the French Revolution, I lie awake in bed and think about having my head chopped off. I can't sleep, can't get it out of my mind. An ax or a sword chopping my head off and then they stick it on a pole or a spike on London Bridge, or—'' He shuddered. ''I can't think about it up straight, and I can't get it out of my mind. Decapitated. Chopped off. Your head in a basket.'' He shivered in the hot sunlight through the glass. Sweating and shivering. Turned to me. ''Those articles?''

''They're all I asked him about,'' I said. ''I talked to Engberg once about the articles. Then my rich dart player appeared with his muscle, and Engberg tried to kill me. Does the dart player ring any bells?''

Stone stared into space as if he were searching a file. He was. Names, faces, and biographies of the rich, famous, and notorious he carried in his mind. ''There's a shadow, a faint glimmer, but I can't pull him out on what you've given me.''

''I think Engberg put him onto me, but one of his guards was outside Sandra Peterson's door the first night, so he had to have some connection to the four hot kids, at least to Robert Asher, yet he seemed surprised when I told him Asher was dead. Or perhaps only surprised I knew Asher was dead.''

Away from the window, Stone began to pace. ''There's a big story somewhere, I can smell it. You talked to Sandra Peterson about the dart player?''

''She didn't recognize him,'' I said, ''but she wasn't one of the four. Maybe there's some kind of connection between my dart player and their parents—why don't you check into that?''

''Okay,'' Stone said.

''Meanwhile, perhaps Norma Powell can tell us more about him.''

We took one car this time. Mine. All the way up the coast, the hot wind blew in gusts out of the canyons, as if trying to blow us into the sea. The sea itself rolled gray-green and ponderous from the hurricane somewhere down off Baja.

On the barren Ventura street, we parked in front of Norma Powell's cottage. There was no answer to our knocks. The shades were down and the front door was

ocked. The Honda was gone from the side of the house.
The back door wasn't locked.

In the kitchen there was a bowl in the sink, a cup and
saucer on the table, a kettle on the stove, a jar of instant
coffee still open, and a box of cereal on the counter. A car-
ton of milk had been left out.

In the bedroom the closets were all open and empty, the
bureau drawers pulled out and empty.

We walked through all the rooms. Nothing was left in the
cottage that hadn't been rented with it except the food.

"You know the club where she works?" I asked Stone.

"I'll take you there."

It was a plain storefront on the far side of Ventura. In a
two-story yellow brick building on a run-down business
street out of the main downtown area near the Ventura
River. The windows had been blacked over on the inside, the
normal front door replaced by a heavy black portal bright
with brass. The Club Chicago. It was closed.

"She must have a landlord," Stone said.

We drove back to the small cottage on the bare street.
There were no receipts, no canceled checks, no business
cards or letterheads to show who the landlord was. Stone
went out while I sat in the kitchen and thought about Norma
Powell. She had gone with all she had, and gone in a hurry.
But had she gone on her own?

Stone came back. "The neighbors say the owner lives out
of town. There's a manager at a local real-estate office."

HE RECEPTIONIST at the downtown real-estate office told
us that Mr. Marsino handled that particular rental but she
was sorry to say it was already rented. We said we wanted to
talk to Mr. Marsino anyway. She was sorry, but Mr. Marsino was out with a client. Mr. Lago or Mr. Teague handled rentals too, but they were out of town. Mrs. Hart never
handled rentals. Did we want to wait for Mr. Marsino? We
did.

The man who finally came in was short and florid in a wrinkled gray suit. Hot and disgruntled, he took a trip to the washroom at the rear, came out drying his face and looking at least resigned. He listened to the receptionist, put on his smile, and came to meet us. The smile faded a little when he heard what our interest in his rental property was, but not too much. He had some class.

"If Miss Powell's gone, it's news to me. As far as I know she's paid up for a year. She does go away most weekends. Maybe that's all she's done."

"She took everything except the furniture," Stone said.

Marsino shrugged. "What can I tell you? She's paid up for four more months, said nothing to me about leaving."

"Where did she go all those weekends?" I said.

"How would I know?"

"Any special visitors? Anyone who came there regularly?"

"Actually, Mr. Shaw, I know nothing about her. She kept the place clean, didn't bother anyone, and paid the year in advance."

"A model tenant," Stone said.

I said, "She's been in the cottage eight months?"

"About that."

"How did she pay the rent?"

"Check."

"You have a file on her? References?"

He walked to a row of filing cabinets, pulled out a slender folder. There was a copy of the lease signed by Norma Powell, a photocopy of a check for the year's rent drawn on a local Ventura bank, and the rental application listing her previous address as 947 Valley Road, Santa Barbara, and her reference as Mr. and Mrs. Raymond Powell at the same address.

"If she's gone, she's out four months' rent," Marsino said.

I hoped that was the worst of her worries.

"Let us know if you hear from her, okay?" Stone said, giving Marsino his card.

Outside he looked up and down Main Street as if he hoped to see Norma Powell materialize. "What now?"

"Back to the cottage and see if we can turn up anything."

On the quiet street we walked again around to the open rear door. I studied the ground more carefully this time. I saw no marks in the dust or dirt. The kitchen was as we had left it.

"What are we looking for?" Stone said.

"Anything," I said. "Where she went. Did she go on her own, or did someone help her go?"

"You think someone took—"

It was as far as Stone got. The man who came from the living room wore a brown suit, a brown shirt, tan shoes and a yellow tie. A burly, red-faced man. With a gun.

"Against the wall."

I leaned against the kitchen wall. Duncan Stone didn't.

"Who the hell do you think—"

The burly man hit Stone across the face with the heavy magnum. Blood spurted. The man swung him around facing the wall, kicked his legs back. Stone leaned on the wall, his head down. Blood dripped from his mouth to the kitchen floor. The intruder turned to me. "What're you two doin' here?"

"Looking for Norma Powell."

"For what?"

"To ask some questions. What are you after?"

"What questions?"

"About some magazine articles."

He looked at me, then at Duncan Stone—who still leaned with his head down, blood dripping—then back at me again. He didn't know what the word *articles* meant, didn't want to look dumb and ask, was trying to figure out how to handle it.

"Stories about her and the others in *Western Ways* magazine," I said.

His voice was suspicious. "You sayin' they got stories 'bout the Powell broad in some magazine?"

Duncan Stone said, "What do you care? You couldn't read them anyway."

The heavy magnum knocked Stone to the floor.

"Bigmouths," he said. And to me, "What's them stories say?"

I told him what the articles were about. He frowned, shook his head as if whatever he wanted from Norma Powell had nothing to do with the articles.

"Shit," he said.

"Maybe we can work together," I said. "You know where she is now? Where she's gone? Where she might go?"

I watched the confusion on his face. He had been planning to ask me the same questions. He didn't like being confused. It made him think someone was trying to fool him. He didn't like people trying to fool him. But he didn't see what I gained by fooling him now—that confused him even more, and that made him uneasy. When he felt uneasy, he snarled with bravado and escaped the situation any way he could think of.

"Maybe I do, maybe I don't, right?" He backed toward the rear door. "You just forget all about Norma Powell, right? You forget an' you don't get hurt, right?" And backed on out of the cottage in approved movie-gunman fashion.

The trouble with the influence of movies and television is that the real gunmen begin to imitate the actors who are supposed to be imitating them until no one knows what is real and what is theater. Soon real life will be exactly like television. A coast-to-coast sitcom. Then television will really be like real life. Or something.

I bent down over Duncan Stone.

"Dunc?"

He opened one eye and looked up at me. "Gone?"

"He's gone."

He sat up. "The son of a bitch." His lips were already swollen, his speech thick. "I guess I wouldn't last long in your line of work. At least I had the sense to just lie quiet after he flattened me."

He stood up, touched his face where the gunman had split his lip, cut the bridge of his nose, loosened some teeth. He felt his head.

"I'll take you to a hospital to get x-rayed," I said.

"Make it down in Malibu," he said. "They know me and I can grab a taxi home."

"You're sure you want to wait until then?"

"I'm sure," he said. "Who the hell was he?"

"We better find out," I said. "After we do what we came back to do."

We searched the cottage thoroughly this time but came up just as empty. There was nothing to show where Norma Powell had gone, or whether she'd gone on her own or had some "help."

"I'll drop you at the Malibu Hospital," I said, "then I'll check at the Santa Monica rooming house, see if they know our friendly gunman."

When we got back to my car, both tires on the right side were flat. They had been slashed with a knife.

"Sweet guy," Stone said through his swollen lips.

It took me over an hour to take one tire off, put on the spare, take the other off, leave the car on the jack and roll both tires to a service station half a mile away. The damage was too extensive to fix, so I had to buy two new tires, roll them back to the car, put them on, return the spare to its place, and finally start south.

The burly, red-faced man was no brain trust, but he was smart enough to immobilize pursuit for a few hours. Or maybe he'd done it just for fun.

FIFTEEN

POLICE CARS WERE parked all along the Santa Monica street in front of the old Victorian rooming house. I found a space up the block and walked back. Police swarmed over the porch and across the grounds. A patrolman stopped me as I climbed the steps.

"You got business?"

"I came to see the Hartmanns. They own the place."

The patrolman turned toward the house. "Hey, Mendoza! Guy out here wants to see the old feller and his wife."

"Who the hell is he?"

The patrolman said, "Who the hell are you?"

"Paul Shaw."

The patrolman yelled, "Paul Shaw!"

There was a silence. A trim, youthful man in gray slacks and a tweed jacket with an open white sport shirt came out of the house and stood on the porch to look down at me.

"You left that note last night?"

I'd forgotten the note. "I wanted to talk to them last night, but they were out. I'd like to talk to them now."

"About what?" His hair was very short in Marine Corps fashion. He stared down at me like a drill instructor.

"A case I'm on." I held out my card. "Thayer, Shaw and Delaney. We're private investigators."

He didn't take the card. "Tell me about the case."

I told him. He wrote some notes.

"LAPD knows about me and the case," I said.

"Good for them," he said. "Now beat it. To New York or L.A., I couldn't care less."

He walked back into the house. The patrolman was enjoying it all. Some policemen are like that. Some whole departments. The power goes to their heads. Mostly in the smaller cities and towns. All in all, it doesn't happen as often as it could.

I went back to my car. An ambulance arrived, and someone was carried from the house on a gurney. I sat and smoked and watched the police wander around the old house, lean out windows, shout to each other and the ramrod Detective Mendoza. Some of the tenants were allowed into the house after Mendoza had talked to them on the porch. Older people, they were nervous. Whatever had happened in the rooming house, the Santa Monica Police weren't treating it lightly. Then, Detective Mendoza wouldn't treat jaywalking lightly.

A man had tried to kill me last night, had died himself with his head torn from his body, and I had needed Sandra Peterson. All that hadn't made a restful sleep, so I dozed behind the wheel until the police began to leave. The patrol cars left one by one, like a military unit pulling out of a captured village. Last to leave, like a good commander, Mendoza gave final instructions to the patrolman who would guard the front door.

I drove around the block, parked on the next street. After working my way through backyards to the rear of the rooming house, I used my keys on the back door and stood listening in the deserted kitchen. I checked the front hall. No police. The living room and dining room were empty.

The brass fittings shone on the Hartmanns' door. I got no answer to my knocks. The door was unlocked. There was no one in the tiny living room, but the police had been there—everything had been moved and very little had been put back in place. I moved some obstructing chairs and opened the bedroom door.

The feisty old man sat in the bed propped up against the headboard. There was a small bandage on his face above the right eye. He didn't move. I walked closer to the bed. His eyes were closed.

"No," the old man said. "Please."

His voice seemed to cringe. I stood at the bed. The bandage was little more than a Band-Aid. His wounds were inside.

"Please. Don't."

"Mr. Hartmann? Max? It's Paul Shaw. The private detective who was here yesterday?"

His head moved vaguely, like the head of a blind insect. Lost inside a sudden reality of fear.

"The detective who asked about the four kids who got in trouble last year?" I said.

He went rigid against the headboard. "I told him. He wouldn't leave her alone." His voice rose, almost hysterical. "Don't touch her! I'll tell. I'll tell!"

I walked around the bed closer to him. "It's all right. He's not here. He can't hurt you now."

He shrank away. "I tried. Too big. Too strong. Wouldn't leave her alone."

"Who, Max?"

"She had to fight! Tell him, I said. Tell him. But she wouldn't tell. She wouldn't."

"Tell who, Max?"

"Big. Red face. Brown suit and a gun. Laughed when he hit her. Every time he laughed!"

"When?" I said. "When was he here?"

"Laughed all the time she screamed."

"When was he here, Max? The man who beat Mabel?"

"Mabel?" His eyes opened, looked up at me. "He beat Mabel."

"Was it today? This afternoon?"

His eyes moved again to look past me toward the window with its shades drawn, as if to know what time it was now. He sat that way for a moment, back still rigid against the headboard, then let his eyes stare again at nothing.

"Morning. He hit me. He hit Mabel. I told her to tell him. She wouldn't. He hit her a long time. Where were they? Drake. Brownlee. Norma Powell. Mabel screamed. I told him. He laughed. He hit her. She wouldn't wake up. I called the police. She just lay there. I called the police, but she just lay there.''

The Hartmanns had known Norma Powell was in Ventura. I bent closer to the old man.

"Doreen Connors, Max. Was she with the other four? Did she come here with them? What happened to her?''

"Doreen?" He frowned into the dim room. "She lived here. From somewhere back east. When they came. She liked Drake. Maybe Brownlee. Someone.''

"Why wasn't she arrested with them?''

"Gone. Moved out. Before.''

"She moved before they did anything?''

"Never came around again.''

"Where did she go?''

He shook his head.

"She left on her own?''

"Everyone helped. The four. Took her things.''

"No forwarding address? Mail?''

"Sent some back. Kids move out—no address, just gone.''

Flotsam and jetsam in single rooms. The broken eggs of a society. The butterflies that blow past on the wind. No known address.

"Brownlee's address," I said. "The one you and Mabel were going to get for me.''

"Told him. Told him everything.''

"Brownlee's new address? What is it?''

He shook his head. "What kind of animal.''

"Brownlee's address," I said.

"Told him. Brownlee. Hermosa Beach. I told!''

"Where in Hermosa Beach?''

Shook his head, his mind lost in another place.

"Brownlee, Max. Hermosa Beach. The street? House number?''

"Pelican Lane, Hermosa Beach.''

And suddenly he was crying. Silent tears down his old face, pale now, not florid and alive anymore. Pale and empty.

"What number, Max?"

He shook his head, cried in the dim room. "What do I do? You know? What do I do?"

"Pelican Lane," I said. "Hermosa Beach. What number?"

"Fifteen." He looked at me for the first time with eyes that seemed to see me. "I told him everything."

"We'll get him," I said.

He looked away toward the dark wall on the far side of the bed. "If she dies, what do I do?"

I sat there in the dim room with him for a time. An old man alone.

SIXTEEN

IN LOS ANGELES a straight line is never the shortest distance between two points. I took the Santa Monica Freeway to the San Diego Freeway and got off on Artesia Boulevard into Hermosa Beach. The burly gunman in brown and yellow had Hal Brownlee's address, and if he'd gone straight from Ventura to Hermosa Beach, I could be too late already.

Pelican Lane turned out to be a short street with alleys behind the houses. Not far from the ocean, number 15 was a three-story gray frame house that had been turned into six apartments. Open decks, with connecting stairs, had been built for each story so that all the apartments could be entered from the outside. In the rear, the names Hal Brownlee and Eliot Drake were listed next to 3B. I rang the downstairs bell, got no answer from the apartment above, but did from the alley.

"You looking for anyone special?"

He was a short young man with wiry black hair, a bland, featureless face, and the beginning of a pot belly that hung over his shorts. He wore an expression of perpetual uncertainty. His shoulders were narrow and his legs shapeless. He was washing a red Jensen-Healy sportcar, held a hose as he looked at me.

"Hal Brownlee," I said. "You know him?"

"He's me. I mean, I'm him."

It was half an admission and half an eager statement. As if he was afraid someone wanted him and hoped to be wanted by anyone. He watched me with the hose in his hand still running.

"Nice car," I said.

"My roomie's," Brownlee said in an envious yet resigned tone of voice, as if he knew he would never be worthy of such a car.

"Why don't you turn the hose off?" I said. "Maybe we can talk."

He looked down at the hose in his hand. "Oh, sorry." And turned it off.

"Thanks. My name's Paul Shaw. I'm a private investigator, working on a case that seems to be connected to your arrest on the drug charge."

"Oh," he said.

I heard the disappointment in his voice. He'd been hoping I was the carrier of something good for him. One of those kids with neither talent nor real ambition who keep hoping that something good will be thrust upon them. With no idea of what that good could be, except that it would make people notice them and life wonderful.

"How long have you and Drake lived here?" I asked.

"Since we got out of jail. We both got jobs in the car wash up on Artesia while we waited for the trial, you know? If we'd known it was gonna take this long, we'd have tried for better jobs, I guess. I mean, it's nice here. We both like the beach."

It was as good an explanation as any for why two college men were working in a car wash in Hermosa Beach.

"What about Norma Powell and Robert Asher? When did you see them last?"

"Hey, not since we got out of jail." Somewhere near there was a violent squeal of brakes and the rending crash of metal. Freeway music. We both waited for the follow-up sounds: the far-off excited voices, the distant beginning wail of sirens. Brownlee seemed to listen to the sirens. "We kind of lost touch, I guess. Eliot didn't want any part of Robbie Asher and his new wife, and Norma always did her own thing. She never did like to say what she was up to."

"That's not how she sounds in the *Western Ways* articles."

"Yeah, I know."

"You've read the articles."

"Sure. Me and Eliot both. Eliot laughed like hell."

"Why? Aren't the articles accurate?"

"Oh, most of what happened is all right. Only it's kind of twisted around, you know? I mean, none of what we did was Robbie Asher's idea. He was just Norma's boyfriend, followed her around most of the time, did just about everything she wanted. Most of what we did was Eliot's or Norma's idea. They were always arguing, Eliot and Norma, and me and Robbie went along with whatever they came up with. Those dumb articles make it look like Robbie made all the plans. Crazy."

"What about Doreen Connors?"

"Doreen?" His pale eyes brightened, his face almost wistful. "Hey, I'd forgotten about her. She was kind of nice. But she was only around a little while. We met her at the rooming house. She sort of took up with Eliot, but she walked out before we pulled the big deal. Eliot said she got scared about the scam, got mad at him, and went off chasing some other guy."

"What other—"

The man who came around the garage wore a car-wash attendant's uniform. Tall and handsome, blond and confident, he was probably the same age as Brownlee, but he moved with the authority of someone a lot older. Some people are born old, born understanding their society, knowing what has to be done to triumph in it, use it, bend it, be a winner.

"Eliot said what about what?" the newcomer said to Brownlee, but his eyes watched me. Dark blue eyes that never blinked. Intimidating. But I've never been intimidated by blond kids, no matter how confident. He blinked first, looked away.

Brownlee said, "I was telling Mr. Shaw about Doreen." He was both eager and uneasy, like a dog with a stern master.

"What about Doreen?" Eliot Drake said. "And who's Mr. Shaw?" He put a sneer into his voice, tried to recover the points he had lost when I outstared him.

I smiled. "Paul Shaw," I said pleasantly. "Thayer, Shaw and Delaney, private investigators. You must be Eliot Drake."

Brownlee sensed the contest, was nervous. "I was just saying Doreen was your girl, El, we only met her at the rooming house, and she split before we tried the big score."

Drake sneered. "Wanted to be my girl, you mean. Sure, I gave her a break for a while, but the deal scared her to death, so she ran. Just a boarding-house kid in over her head. With the score and with me."

He laughed at his joke, but it wasn't really a joke. He believed he was much too much for a "boarding-house kid."

"You know where I can reach Miss Connors?" I asked.

"Hell, no. She just flew the coop. When it got tough down in the dirt with the big boys. She had the hots for the wild scene, little old Doreen, but she couldn't cut the mustard. Strictly lace-curtain, a parlor radical. When it got to the nitty-gritty, she was a blob, jellyfish time. So she ran back somewhere south of Succotash."

The hyped-up speech had a powerful aura of submerged violence. Even in the car-wash uniform there was a sense of danger about Eliot Drake, the manic assurance of a born leader. Charisma.

"You've read those *Western Ways* articles?"

"Fairy tales." His laugh and sneer came together this time. "But they got all our names right, so what the hell. If they want to make old Norma into Snow White with the three big bad wolves, why not? Maybe it builds sympathy for all of us. Let the bleeding-hearts have a field day. It could get us off light."

"Norma was no Little Red Riding Hood?"

"Almost as tough as me," Drake said.

"Asher didn't coerce her into joining you all?"

"Other way around. She brought him in, and he trotted after like a damn puppy. Norma got tired of him, let him know it too. That's when he picked up with some punk broad, Sandra something, brought her around once or twice before Norma and I told him to cool it with the outsiders until after the deal went down. Then he could flake off with anyone he wanted. Me and old Norma were cozying by then anyway. She said she liked my power. I kind of liked her power." He winked at me, tossed his blond hair. He liked himself. A lot.

"Maybe Norma was why Doreen ran off."

"Could be," Drake agreed. "You have a glass jaw, you better stay out of the ring."

The mishmash speech of mixed slangs and metaphors was his gimmick, his trademark. Behind it the diction and grammar were all college and prep school. Jazzed-up hype over a quick, educated mind. Everyone has a disguise of some kind.

"So the pieces in *Western Ways* are slanted to make Norma Powell look like an innocent corrupted by the wrong man or men. Any ideas why?"

"No," Hal Brownlee said quickly. He hadn't said much since Drake arrived. I had the feeling he never said much after Drake arrived. Probably no one did. But he spoke up now, and fast.

"Why do you care, Shaw?" Drake said. "What's a private cop doing chasing around after a bungled caper a year ago? We have to be old history."

"To me and the cops, but not to someone." I told them about the murder of Robert Asher, about the burly gunman who liked to beat up people, and about the dart player. "Someone killed Asher, someone's looking for Norma and you two, and someone doesn't like me asking questions."

They both stood silent in the September sun with the hot wind blowing debris along the alley behind the houses. Brownlee was pale, looked up and down the alley for a killer to appear. He had a basically simple mind. Drake only looked thoughtful.

"Either of you know the gunman or the dart player?"

"No," Brownlee said, shook his head vigorously.

"Whatever they want," Drake said, "it's not us."

The sounds of traffic were close by on the avenues, the cries of swimmers and volleyball players on the beach.

"That gunman knows where you live," I said.

"If he shows," Drake said, "we tell him he's made a mistake and it's all cool. We don't need a private cop."

"If he shows, you'll need anyone you can get."

"We can take care of ourselves," Drake said.

He probably believed it. Brownlee didn't look as sure.

"If someone killed Robbie Asher," Drake said, "it's got nothing to do with us. Probably not even connected to our caper. Go look into the punk scene, that broad he married. We've got a trial and a rap to beat."

I left them by the half-washed car in the alley. Brownlee still held the hose in his hand.

I drove back toward Artesia Boulevard and the San Diego Freeway. At the first corner a crowd filled the sidewalks. It was the car crash I'd heard earlier. Two motorcycles half-blocked the street, and a single car was up on the sidewalk, its hood barely buckled against a brick wall, a small dent in the right side. Not much of an accident.

But I stopped. A man sat in the front seat of the car on the sidewalk. His head was slumped on the steering wheel at an odd angle. An impossible angle, and there was something familiar about the man.

I parked and walked back to look. The man in the car was dead, his neck broken. He was the burly, red-faced gunman in the brown suit and yellow tie.

SEVENTEEN

"HIS NECK SNAPPED as cold as Monday leftover chicken."

Lieutenant Jacoby of the Hermosa Beach Police was a skinny man who talked with his hands. He didn't like the whole damn setup with the dead gunman, not in his jurisdiction. Beach riots he understood, but this? "Died instantly, coroner says. Not a mark on him. His license says he was Jay Norca from Victorville. The Victorville cops tell me the address is a phony and they don't know him, and you tell me he was gunning for someone. He was carrying a magnum, ammo, and a nasty knife up a sleeve."

I sat in Jacoby's office with half the day gone and a cheap hamburger like lead in my stomach. Something I'd had sent in while I waited for Jacoby to get around to listening to me.

"I don't think it was an accident, Lieutenant."

"Accident?" His arm swept the air. "Good Christ, no, it wasn't any accident. A nickel fender-bender like that? No bruises to show impact enough to break his smile, much less his neck? Of course it's not an accident. It's murder straight out, only it stinks. Someone wanted to make it look like an accident, but they loused it up something awful."

"They?" I said.

He got up, paced, waved. "Who breaks the neck of a gunman like that without leaving a mark on him? No struggle at all. Not one killer, no sir. Not amateurs, neither. It's got all the aroma of an organized mob killing, and we ain't had a gangster killing around here since I joined the force."

"For gangsters, they didn't do a very good job."

"Who the hell ever told you professional crooks were any good at killings? Half the time they screw it up royally. It's cold-blooded, a royal bungle, and had to be more than one guy. That sounds like underworld soldiers, not a contract hit. Cheap muscle ought to be cutting salami instead of killing."

"Maybe just out of practice," I said. "You know any underworld mobs around Hermosa Beach?"

"No, but I don't know Norca neither." He paced, gestured in anger to some unseen enemy in the small office, and then sat down again. "Norca's identification is a dead end, and that means he didn't want anyone to know what he did or where he hung his hat. I've got his prints in Sacramento and Washington. My guess is he was up to his wishbone in prior arrests, probably did some time." He scowled at his own hands playing with a pencil, then at me. "Tell me again what you knew about him."

"He was somehow connected to the four kids waiting for trial in the drug case. He was after Norma Powell up in Ventura, and I think he came to Hermosa Beach to find the other two."

"And ended up dead," Jacoby said. "Before or after he found your boys?"

"That's a good question. Drake wasn't around at first, showed up after I heard the 'accident' in the distance."

Jacoby shook his head. "No way a kid killed Norca alone, but we'll talk to your Drake and Brownlee. Thanks for coming and telling me about it. You didn't have to. Leave your office number in case I turn up something you can use."

I drove back to Hollywood in the late-afternoon traffic, which was bumper-to-bumper and moving viciously in the hot wind. Once, back before Vietnam, when I was still trying to be an actor and dazzle the world, I drove all alone at dawn on a long highway under an empty sky with nothing in sight except the road and the universe. That's something the millions who drive only in Los Angeles or New York, Chicago or Houston, will never know. It's something I'd like to experience once more before I die, maybe with Maureen, but my chances get less every year as the real-estate men and the developers change the face of the country.

IN OUR OFFICE Mildred held out a *Los Angeles Times*.

"Duncan Stone called. He said to look at the entertainment section. An ad."

In Los Angeles the entertainment section is a large section. The ad Stone meant was on page four. A small ad for an out-of-town nightclub: The Club Chicago in Ventura. It announced that J.C. Connors, in her first West Coast engagement in ten years, was appearing nightly.

EIGHTEEN

THE CLUB CHICAGO was open, but the first show would not go on until 8:00 P.M., and J.C. Connors saw no one before a show. I remembered how it feels before you go on. How you have to be alone to face yourself. Not a lot different from the hours before going out on search and destroy in Nam.

I sat at the bar and had a Beck's. The barman who served me wore a suit and tie, looked at his watch every minute, and had to search under the bar for a towel to wipe his hands.

"Owner?" I asked.

He nodded, looked at his watch again. "Fifth goddamn time this month the bartender's late. You tend bar? Say yes and you got a job."

"Not this year," I smiled. "Your singer going to show?"

"That you can put in the bank. She's a pro. Still don't know why J.C. Connors wanted to play a joint in the boonies, but I don't ask any questions, right?"

"She asked to sing here?"

"Called from New York. Could I use her for a month or so? Could I use J.C. Connors? I told her write her own ticket, except for the pay. In this nowheresville I got a limit. She said the nut didn't matter, and sure enough she showed up first week in August, been here ever since. You tell me, right? A headliner like J.C. Connors askin' for this town!"

"Lucky," I said. "Not like the bartender or that waitress you just lost. Or maybe you didn't lose the waitress."

He took out a Beck's, opened it, drank from the bottle, looked at it in his hand as if he knew he shouldn't drink beer.

"What waitress is that?"

"Norma Powell."

"Who are you, mister? What do you want with Norma?"

I told him. Who I was and what I wanted with Norma Powell. I know surprise when I see it, even when it tries to hide behind a bottle of beer. Especially when it tries to hide.

"Out on bail? All year?"

"And going to trial soon."

"Selling drugs? Pills?"

I said, "I think someone doesn't want her to go on trial. One way or the other."

He put the beer bottle down. "She's in danger?"

"She could be."

He smiled, picked up the beer, and drank as if it suddenly tasted better. As if I'd brought him good news. I had.

"So that's why she took off! I should've known it was something big, important, you know? I mean, we'd gotten pretty close. It didn't figure she'd just walk out."

I'd given him an explanation for Norma Powell's walking away from the club, and from him. Something he could accept. It was okay. She was in danger, scared, it hadn't been anything to do with him. There was nothing wrong with him.

"We were really into something," he said. He got two more Beck's, opened them, didn't take my money. We were friends. "She's one exciting woman for her age. Smart, too, picked up the club business fast. I gave her a couple of raises, and she was in line for hostess. She had a great future around here, I told her. Not just in the club, if you know what I mean. That's why it didn't figure when she didn't show for work. I mean, I knew we had more than just some rolls in the hay, you know? Now I get it. Look, what can I do to help Norma?"

"You can tell me where she might go."

A heavy man tying on a white apron hurried from somewhere in the rear of the club. The owner scowled at him, but the bartender quickly busied himself, and the owner had me to answer.

"Her cottage is all I know. She never talked about the past."

People were coming in now. The hostess hustled them to tables. Waiters appeared to take their drink orders before they sat down. The owner seemed to count the crowd, or maybe he was looking for Norma Powell. They'd had a romance going, the owner and Norma—a torrid one, from the sound of his voice when he talked about her. I wondered if Norma's voice would be as torrid. She had told him nothing about her past, and less about her future. It didn't sound exactly like a deep relationship, at least for her.

The owner drained his bottle. "Look, when you find Norma, tell her Barney wants to help her. Anything she needs. And her job's open anytime. You tell her."

"I'll tell her."

He stopped to say something to the tardy bartender. The bartender made an obscene gesture behind his back. I watched the tables fill with people. They all sat facing the small bandstand at the far end of the long room. I didn't have to wonder what had brought J.C. Connors to California.

At exactly 8:00 P.M. she appeared from a corner doorway. One moment there was only the piano and the waiting crowd, and then she was there. Black satin jump suit, low black high-heeled boots, black gloves, a black turtleneck—all against her mannish silver-blond hair and pale face, a single narrow silver cord that circled her waist. Like a shadow, she moved to the silent piano without looking right or left, sat at the keys head down. A single spotlight picked her out of the darkness of the crowded room. A small woman with a soft face and slim figure and an absorption in her work that made the packed room quiet. She waited until the final small noise silenced.

Then she began to sing. In a low, clear blues voice with no hint of sentimentality, only a sadness.

She sang of life not especially good nor exceptionally bad. The way it is for most of us who want more than we have, what we have never had and probably never will have; but life isn't worth much if we can't go on hoping, pretending. The stuff of small dreams. The possible if not probable. An austere style that held the audience in utter silence, with only muted murmurs of approval between numbers, as if she were a kind of priest at a kind of ceremony. She held them, us, by the reality, the honesty. She sang of life the way it had to be, of real life, and the audience listened and heard and perhaps even understood.

The set was short, half an hour. Then she bowed once and smiled her only smile. A small smile that seemed to say she sang only what we, her listeners, really knew better than she did. I got up to go backstage when she appeared at the corner of the bar near me. She stood almost totally in shadow, unnoticed by the crowd now released from her silence. She leaned against a bar stool, drank from a shot glass and a tall glass of water.

"You sing well," I said.

"Thanks." She remembered me.

"You knew more about Norma Powell than just a letter."

"Not until I came out here. I got lucky, found where she was, took this job."

"You knew about the four in the rooming house with Doreen."

She drank. "No. I found the rooming house through Norma Powell after I met her here. I found out about the four of them only yesterday morning from the Hartmanns." She sipped her water. "Where is Norma now?"

"I was going to ask you."

She shook her head. "I went to her cottage today to look for her, but it's cleaned out."

"You know a heavy, red-faced man in a brown suit and yellow tie? Ever see him around Norma Powell?"

"No. Should I have seen him?"

"I'm glad you didn't."

"Why?"

I told her why, and what had happened to the gunman. I told her about Drake and Brownlee. She drank her whiskey, chased it down with the water. I drank my beer.

"You think this gunman scared her away?" she said.

"He was looking for her. Probably for Brownlee and Drake, too. Maybe for Asher. Maybe for Doreen."

"Where are they? Brownlee and Drake?"

"Hermosa Beach." I gave her the address. "They say they don't know where Doreen is now. She left the rooming house before their big plan went into action."

She finished her whiskey, nodded to the bartender. He brought her shot and my Beck's. She drank with her eyes half-closed, enjoying the whiskey.

I said, "You've been out here in a two-bit club for over a month just to get near Norma Powell. That's a lot of sacrifice for a New York headliner. To locate a grown daughter who stopped writing over a year ago. I mean, why the big effort when you didn't do much to find her for a whole year?"

She drank, sipped water. "Does that mean something?"

"It means I think you're worried about a lot more than losing touch."

For a time she watched the desperate revelers at the crowded tables. Then she took a cigarette from the gold and black case, gave me one, sat down on the bar stool. I lit the cigarettes.

"Doreen ran away from home two years ago." She blew smoke into the thick haze of the club. "From me, I suppose. Too busy, too self-centered, too involved with my own marvelous talent. Or maybe not. I don't really know what made her run away. I won't until I find her, if then. She came out to L.A. Where else, right? A show-business mother: N.Y. to L.A." She drank. "By the time I heard from her, she'd moved in with a man called Jack. Just Jack, and a box number in Hollywood. She said Jack didn't know about me, didn't want her writing to anyone. She was in love with him, but he was a lot older, violent and unpredictable, sometimes mean. It sounded to me as if she was as scared of him as in love with him.'' She drank again. By now she'd stopped bothering with the water. "He was away a lot, came and went when it suited him, from what I could tell. So she began hanging around the punk scene.''

She emptied her shot glass, nodded again to the bartender. "Then I got a letter maybe a month before her last one. She'd left Jack, moved into a rooming house, and met another guy. His name was Eliot, and she was crazy about him, and he didn't sound any better to me than Jack except perhaps younger and classier. She still didn't give me any last name or an address. The same P.O. box. I guess she still wasn't sure of me, wanted to keep contact but not have me breathing down her neck, and for a while her letters were a lot brighter.'' She stopped to motion again to the bartender, who didn't seem to have seen her wave for a refill. "Then I got the last letter. She was all the way down again. Depressed and scared. Jack was back in the picture, and she was really scared. She said she might even be coming home. Maybe soon. Even if she didn't come home, she'd have to move again, and she'd write when she got settled.'' She lifted her shot glass to drink. It was still empty. She stared at it, then at the bartender at the far end of the bar. "That was the last time I heard from her.''

She stared toward the bartender. The owner had come out of the door marked *Private* and was walking to the bar. She watched the owner. "My letters were returned, the box had lapsed. I waited almost a year, then I came out. All I had to go on were two first names, a P.O. box, and Norma Powell. I showed Doreen's picture at the Hollywood post office. They recognized her, but no one knew when she'd stopped coming in. The box had lapsed because she hadn't paid. Then I asked them about Norma Powell and got lucky. One of them had read *Western Ways* and remembered the name. The guy on the pop-music and club beat at that magazine is an old friend, so I had lunch and he told me where I could find Norma Powell. I went back to New York, called the owner of this trap, closed my Vanguard run, and came out. Norma eventually talked about that rooming house. You told me about the four of them and the big drug scheme, but I still haven't found anything about where Doreen is."

The owner stood behind us. J.C. didn't turn around. She said, "I'll have another bourbon."

"After the last show," the owner said.

She watched him in the bar mirror. "You think I can't do my job?"

"If you didn't feel this club was good enough, you shouldn't have taken the job."

"Who the hell are you to tell me I'm drinking too much?"

"The owner of this club."

She turned on the stool to look up at him. "One more won't hurt me. I need it, Barney."

"After the last show you can get stoned."

"Maybe there won't be any damned last show!"

"Then you won't work in this state again." He touched her thin shoulder in the black satin jumpsuit. "You're the best I ever had in this club, don't ruin it."

She stood and walked away toward the bandstand and the waiting piano. The owner watched her go.

"What's her trouble?" he said. "You know, Shaw?"

"No," I said.

The room silenced, and J.C. Connors began to sing again. Some lost song about lost people in a lost voice.

I left. If the owner wanted to know her trouble, he would have to ask her himself. I wasn't even sure I knew. She'd told me a lot, but not all. She hadn't really answered my question—why had she waited a whole year to start looking for Doreen?

NINETEEN

As I Crested the Conejo Grade into the Conejo Valley, the hot wind carried the odor of smoke. The fearful odor of burning that causes all eyes in Southern California to turn from whatever they are doing to search the nearest dry hills, the horizon.

Far off in the night I saw the faint glow of flames high on the darker shadows of the mountains. All the way to Hollywood I watched the glow spread through some remote canyon. The odor of smoke hung faint in the air even in Hollywood, and people on the street walked looking up and out toward the mountains. I drove up the winding drive to Sandra Peterson's apartment. The rail that had killed Murray Engberg was still bent. Sandra opened the door.

"I had to go to work," she said. "We've got a fire over toward Santa Monica."

"I saw," I said as I went in. "A big, burly, red-faced man who favors brown suits with yellow ties and carries a gun. Mean anything to you?"

"No." She left the door open in the heat, sat looking up at me from the shabby couch in the tiny living room. She wore a purple jump suit this time, tight and curved. The low black boots. Fanned herself with a black and gold fan. "Did you find out anything about the rich man in the limousine?"

"Not yet." I stood near the window, where I could get what air there was. Somehow, it wasn't the same as last night. "I found Brownlee and Drake, lost Norma Powell. That gunman in brown was looking for all of them, too, but someone broke his neck in Hermosa Beach. Drake could have killed him, but not alone. He knew three of them, probably all four. He could have been looking for Asher, and found him. He carried a knife.''

She stopped fanning herself, as if she no longer felt the heat. ''How did he know them all?''

''Yes, how.'' I watched the view. ''The girl who introduced you to your husband, Doreen Connors, had a boyfriend named Jack before she took up with Eliot Drake at the rooming house. She was around the punk scene before she went to the rooming house. When you first met Doreen, was there anyone named Jack?''

''Not that I remember. She hung out with a different group than I did.''

''Are any of them still around?''

''I think so, yes.''

''Will they talk to me?''

''Not if you went alone.''

''You want to take me?''

''Tonight?''

''The sooner the better.''

''All right,'' she said. ''Paul?''

''Later,'' I said. I turned from the window. ''Okay?''

She nodded, smiled. ''Okay. I'll change.''

While she changed, I called Duncan Stone to check in. He didn't answer. I hung up, thought about Sandra Peterson. And about Maureen. Sometimes marriages change. Most of the time. And we don't live in an age when our very physical survival depends on a man having a woman in his house or garden, a woman having a man in the fields or forests. Bertrand Russell once said there can be such a thing as too much freedom. And where was Duncan Stone at almost 11:00 P.M.?

I tried his number again, let the phone ring longer this time. I heard the receiver lift, the ringing stop. A numbing crash deafened me. The receiver had been dropped. I listened to silence.

Not silence; breathing. Slow breathing.

''Duncan?''

The almost silent breathing, harsh and labored, and a sharp tap...tap...tap...tap...

"Duncan? Who's there?"

Only the so-slow breathing and the tap...tap..., and then nothing. Silence. I hung up the phone. Sandra came out of the bedroom. She had her wig on, her spiked blond hair tipped purple, wore black leotard tights, the boots, a ragged man's shirt two sizes too big and belted with a leather garrison belt. I mopped my neck just looking at her.

I said, "We're going by way of Malibu."

In my car I took my little Colt Agent from under the seat, clipped the holster to my belt in back. The smell of smoke was stronger on the Hollywood Freeway. By the time we were halfway to the sea on the Santa Monica Freeway, I could see narrow tendrils of flame licking up over a distant ridge of the Santa Monica Mountains. Even the ocean didn't bring the cool air it usually does, and we drove on up the Coast Highway into Malibu with gusts of hot wind from the canyons shaking the car.

Stone's green MG was parked behind his beach house. The hood was cold. The fence gate was ajar.

"Stay in the car. Lock the doors."

He lay on the floor of his large living room with its vast view of the sea and dark sky. Beside the dangling telephone receiver. He'd been beaten. Both eyes bloody and swollen closed. His nose and jaw broken. One arm twisted in an impossible angle. Bloody but alive. I called the paramedics and the police.

Then I sat on the floor with him and held his hand. He was unconscious, but perhaps somewhere deep inside he knew he was no longer alone. I sat there wiping the sweat from his face until the paramedics arrived.

Sandra came in with them. I stood aside with her, let them work, studied the big room. There was no sign of a fight, nothing disturbed. A pencil lay between Stone's hand and the telephone. Barely conscious, unable to speak, he had crawled to the ringing phone, knocked the receiver to the floor, and tapped on it with the pencil to tell me to come.

A Deputy Welch was in charge of the team from the Malibu sheriff's station. Despite the heat, he was almost as neat in his gray suit as the uniformed deputies.

"He's been working with me," I said, and told my story again. "It started as an LAPD case, moved into Santa Monica, Hermosa Beach, and now Malibu."

"You're saying it's all one case, Shaw?"

"I think so."

"We know Stone out here. You're sure this wasn't about one of his stories? Some dirt he was digging into?"

"No, I'm not sure."

They took our names and addresses, and after the paramedics had taken Stone to the hospital, let us go with instructions to be available whenever he regained consciousness. If he did.

In the car I asked, "Where do we go?"

"Back to Hollywood. Danny's Hot Dogs. We call it Oki Dog, and it's a hangout."

The fire was still only a few thin fingers of far-off flame and a glow in a canyon as we drove back along the Santa Monica Freeway to the Hollywood and on into Hollywood itself.

TWENTY

ON SANTA MONICA Boulevard, Danny's Hot Dogs was an ordinary fast-food stand with serving windows and a covered patio eating area. It was late, but the heat had brought out a crowd gathered around the windows and tables, eating and talking. Mostly talking. Loud, violent talk, as if they were all furious at each other, but it was only the world they were angry with.

Sandra took me to an empty table. We sat down.

"What do we do?"

"We wait for people to show. Christian Death and Black Flag are playing over in Costa Mesa, so a lot aren't here. We'll give it an hour, then go over to Costa Mesa."

The small crowd was dressed primarily in black, links of chain around most necks. Swastikas abounded: on T-shirts and jackets, tattooed on arms, not all male. The men had shaved skulls, sported Mohawk roaches, or at least had the sides shaved and the top spiked. The women wore their hair short and dyed any color they could think of from purple to silver.

"What do they do besides eat hot dogs and dye their hair?"

"Talk, listen to music, dance. Most of us play guitar or sing. Sometimes I think there're as many punk bands in L.A. as punks. I sing, Robbie was learning guitar. Why not? Everyone says it's better to participate than be a spectator."

As others arrived, Sandra spoke to them about Doreen Connors and Jack. None of them knew anything. They were all loud and belligerent for no particular reason I could see except that I was there. Or maybe it was the heat. Leather can be hot.

"Who the fuck's he?"

"Paul Shaw," Sandra told them. "He's helping me find who killed Robbie."

"Hey, all right. Hell, I remember that Doreen. No older guy shit, you know? Hell, it's more'n a year, you know?"

Many of them remembered Doreen, but no Jack. Most of them were still teenagers, young and clean despite the violent clothes and swagger. They probably lived at home with their parents and kept their rooms neat. They could have been anybody's kids, rich and poor, and almost all were white. A few looked as if they might make the grade as street toughs someday, but most were the angry children of the affluent suburbs.

After an hour of nothing, it was time for Costa Mesa and the concert. Sandra directed me along the freeways and city streets to a rock club called the Cuckoo's Nest. The music pounded my ears as we went in. Guitars in the hands of the punk band up on the stage were like machine guns as the lead singer screamed out the vicious lyrics of a hammering song with such anger the veins bulged in his shaved head. As I watched, he leaped down into the audience to stomp and rage nose to nose with the wildly approving punks. There were perhaps two hundred kids in the club, some fifteen or twenty out on the pit of the dance floor smashing into each other in a ritualized dance known as the Slam.

"Take a table," Sandra said. "I'll be back."

I took a table, waited and watched. This was the violent image that scared the proper people. An image built up by the newspapers, the magazines like *Western Ways*, that had to sell forbidden thrills, vicarious titillations, to build circulation. So they sold a picture of destruction, of concerts more like riots, of anger that said if they could find no values they might as well blow everything away. Nihilism. The protest of nothing.

Was it their fault it seemed so hollow? The empty protest of spoiled brats in a society that offered them ease and comfort undreamed of in most of this world? A society so comfortable their elders could see nothing to protest about, where their fellow teenagers accepted the dreary goals given them, wanted only to go to business school and get rich. They had no Vietnam or civil-rights marches or student protest movements, but only a restless sense that something was wrong with a comfortable world that lived on the pain of others. So they could only protest their world itself, not yet ready to lie down and accept the cocoon of privilege. A tiny group of children who knew that they wanted something different, but had no way of knowing, in a world of comfortable corporate capitalism, what that was.

Sandra returned with an older young woman in torn bib overalls festooned with gold chains, and green dyed hair worn, oddly, medium-long. Among the general run of the shouting mob, she seemed like an old lady.

"Sylvia remembers Doreen and Jack," Sandra said.

"Cylvia with a C," the woman said. "Sure I remember Doreen and Jack. I knew Dorrie since she first came to L.A. Old Jack was her man for a long time. I never did meet him, but I didn't like him sight unseen. She was scared of him, you could see that. He never came around with her. Anyway, she finally got shut of him and moved into a rooming house in Santa Monica. Didn't see much of her for a couple of months after that, so I sort of forgot her. Then she showed up again, and this time she was really scared. I mean terrified out of her pants. She was seeing Jack again, and she was real scared."

"How long had she been back with Jack?"

"It sounded like only a couple of days."

"Did she say where she was living then?"

"Still in that Santa Monica rooming house."

"Did she ever talk about Jack, what he looked like? Anything to identify him?"

"She talked about him all the time, how rough and tough he was, how much 'man,' but she never described him. You could tell he was a lot older, but that's all."

"But she was still living in Santa Monica when she took up with him again."

"The way it sounded."

"That was a year ago?"

"Just about."

We thanked Cylvia, Sandra went off to try to find others who had known Doreen Connors and the elusive Jack, and I watched the teenagers slamming into each other in what was, in the end, just another ritual of passage. By 2:00 A.M. Sandra gave up and we drove back to her apartment. The view hadn't changed, but it was quieter in the small hours, the sparse lights of the traffic on the freeways overshadowed by the wider glow of the fire in the Santa Monica Mountains.

"Paul?"

I watched the distant fire. "We needed each other last night. You just lost a husband, I have a wife in New York I've been married to for twenty years, but we needed each other."

"I want you," Sandra said. "Everything reminds me of Robbie."

"A man tried to kill me. I had his blood on me. I needed someone."

"Robbie's dead. I want someone."

She sat on the shabby old couch they had probably bought together in the feverish days of their beginning, legs close together in the black tights, breasts soft under her tattered shirt, the spiked purple hair of the wig making her look like the teenager she still seemed.

"I don't want to go back to my hotel. I want you. What does that make my marriage?"

"I don't know." She looked up at me. "I don't care."

I came away from the window. "There've always been
women. I don't know why, except that it seems right at the
time."

"Robbie was the only one for a year. I don't know why."

I picked her up then. Held her small and slender. Her lips
strained up to kiss, be kissed. I carried her into the small
bedroom, where the big bed filled the room and looked so
empty. We took off each other's clothes. Kissed breasts and
buttocks that were soft and tight at the same time, necks and
throats and bellies and wet lips. Naked in the hot night, I
pulled her tights down to her knees, her thighs tight together, and entered her slowly. I wanted to make love for a
long time. I needed to. Our needs are what we are, the needs
and what we do about them. After a long time, soaked with
sweat in the stifling night, I took off her tights and we
slipped together.

There was a tinge of dawn when I became aware again of
the traffic below and the distant sound of fire sirens. Dawn
without coolness. Her lips touched my neck, moved away.

"Did Jack kill Robbie, Paul?"

Her face was profiled against the faint lightening outside
the window high in the hills. A thin film of sweat glistened.

"There's some link between that gunman, Jay Norca, and
the four. Maybe Jack's the link. There's more about Doreen than J.C. Connors told me. She went back to Jack
while she was still at the rooming house. While she was still
supposedly in love with Eliot Drake. She went back to Jack
despite being terrified of him, and then she moved out of the
rooming house and hasn't been heard from since."

"Could Jack have killed Norca? Norca and Robbie?"

"It's possible. Or Jack and Jay Norca could be the same
man and there's still a killer out there."

She seemed to shiver in the dark, laid her head against my
shoulder. We slept past sunrise. A dark sun through drifting smoke. Or she slept. I thought about needs and solutions.

Most of us live in a world without the weight of daily survival. Here in America, at least. Fifty percent of marriages end in divorce, the rest struggle to find some necessity or go their separate ways without divorce. Most needs are the same, only the solutions differ. I had my needs and my solutions, and somewhere out there in the sprawling city someone's needs had been solved by two murders, and the brutal beating of Duncan Stone. So far.

TWENTY-ONE

IT WAS TOO hot for coffee, but we had Danish together at an open café on Sunset Boulevard. Smoke hung thick over the Santa Monica Mountains now, and far to the northeast across the Valley another wisp of smoke rose into the streaked sky.

I drove on to our office, watched World War II bombers fly low and ponderous into the distant smoke. It looked like the air raids in the old war movies, but the payload was now a cloud of red chemicals more like my days in Vietnam. Helicopters dashed back and forth across the smoky sky, and every firehouse was empty.

Mildred was at the window watching the distant fire.

"Any calls?" I asked.

"No," she said without turning. "I live near that fire."

In Southern California everyone stands on streets, on patios, at windows, to watch the fire in the hills that could blow in their direction. A land of little rain, of chaparral and mesquite, of thick brush and hot sun, it was intended to burn every ten to twenty years to keep the balance of nature. For the Indians this had been no problem. A grass hut can be rebuilt tomorrow, stone pots are easily carried away on backs.

But for we who crowd up the dry slopes, move high on the waterless mountainsides, the fires are fear and disaster. The more who come, the more fires there are, the more who are burned out. It won't stop until we turn the chaparral into plastic, the mesquite into brick, the oaks into concrete. Only then will the fires stop. When we have made the land into something different from the land that made us come here in the first place.

She turned. "I'm sorry, Paul. It's this weather and the fires. What do you need?"

"Find out all you can about a crook named Jay Norca. Start with LAPD, Sacramento, the FBI, and finish with Lieutenant Jacoby in Hermosa Beach. What was Norca up to the last years, who were his close friends, you know."

I sat at Dick Delaney's desk and called New York. Call it guilt. With the time difference, she should be up but not yet gone to work. She was.

"How's the special going?"

"Lousy, if you care."

"I care."

"Then come home."

"I care too much to come home."

"What devious insight is that?"

"You don't want a doormat for a husband."

"Be here and be a doormat."

"Ask the studio to send you out."

"By then you'll be too busy back here."

"Life is hard."

"It doesn't have to be."

"Yes, it does, one way or the other."

"Maybe I should choose the other way."

"I couldn't stop you."

"Come home."

"Soon."

"If I'm out, I'll leave a note."

She had her needs too, and her solutions. What kind of marriage did I want? What was my solution going to be? I called the Malibu Hospital and asked for Duncan Stone. A casual voice asked my name, and when I'd last seen Mr. Stone.

"Last night. I'm the one who found him, Paul Shaw."

"The peeper?"

"Himself."

"Shit," he said, not so casual.

"How is Stone? Has he said what happened?"

"Ask the sheriff," he snarled, and hung up.

What makes us all so angry? Maybe it's the difference between what we're told to want and what we end up getting.

TWENTY-TWO

ALL THE WAY to Hermosa Beach the smoke blew across a yellowish sky north toward Santa Monica and east behind me in the San Fernando Valley.

There was no answer from the third-floor rear apartment of Drake and Brownlee, no car in the alley or their garage. At the top of the open stairs the apartment door was unlocked. People who live in beach communities have communal minds.

The apartment was typical of any beach town from Alaska to the Gulf. A small living room of mismatched furniture bought at garage and liquidation sales. Large windows with a narrow view of the sea between adjacent houses. Two small bedrooms, little closet space, a narrow kitchen, and a bathroom with an ancient tub, a dripping hot-water faucet, and sand on the floor.

I pawed through the debris of clothes and food containers on the floors, searched the two closets, opened the drawers. I found a thousand dollars' worth of clothes, no books, cracked china, an empty refrigerator, and nothing about the case except all five issues of *Western Ways*. The most recent was open on a table, every reference to Eliot Drake underlined.

After two hours, Drake and Brownlee had not appeared. I used their telephone to call Malibu. Duncan Stone was out of danger, angry, and wanted to see me. The fire in the Santa Monica Mountains was closer as I drove up Highway One past Pacific Palisades. I could see flames inside the smoke blowing toward the ocean on the hot wind. In Malibu they were standing out in the road watching another thin thread of smoke to the east in their mountains.

Duncan Stone lay in the high hospital bed with most of his face hidden by bandages and one baleful eye staring at me. Only the eye moved, an undercurrent of pain in his voice.

"About time."

"You've been busy. What happened, Dunc?"

The single eye clouded but didn't flinch. "I'd been up in Santa Barbara checking on your dart player in the limousine. When I got back to the house, they were waiting. Two of them. Big and fast and efficient. I never saw their faces. No talk, no smiles. Just did their job. They did a real good job."

"You don't know who they were?"

The solitary eye glared. "I didn't see their faces or hear their voices, but I know who they were. I didn't have to see their faces, just had to know where I'd been and what I'd found."

"You found out who the dart player is."

His unbandaged eye brightened fiercely. "Walter Maxwell Hardin. I knew he rang a bell, but he's not L.A., stays out of the papers. Reclusive, behind the scenes. Inherited a financial empire and tripled it. His holdings cover the country, probably the world. Oil to entertainment. Money and power."

"He lives in Santa Barbara?"

"He lives everywhere, but Santa Barbara is where the big house is. The one Daddy left him. Where he started."

His single eye closed. He breathed slowly for a time. I waited. He spoke again without opening the eye.

"I've been thinking. What the hell's a man like Hardin got to do with four punk kids and a two-bit drug scam?"

"Maybe five kids," I said, and told him about Doreen Connors and Jack.

His unbandaged eye blinked. "Paul, listen! The police don't know where the pills those kids sold came from, do they? Hardin owns big chunks of two pharmaceutical firms! I don't remember which, but I'll find out as soon as I'm out of here."

"Pretty small potatoes for a rich man."

"Nothing about money is too small for a rich man."

Before I could answer, the nurse and Sheriff's Deputy Welch came in. The nurse said Stone needed to rest; Welch wanted to know what I'd found out. I gave him a skimmed report of the case so far, a description of the two muscle-men who'd beaten Stone, but not the name of Walter Maxwell Hardin. Stone's unbandaged eye gleamed. Hardin was ours.

"Let's see," Welch said. "Two big musclemen he can't identify but you think could be the same two who grabbed you in Santa Monica. You don't know their names or who they work for, you're not sure where they fit into your case. That about it?"

"About," I agreed.

"Swell," he said. "You'll let us know when you do have some names or connections? Think you could do that?"

"No problem," I said.

Welch growled and left. The nurse folded her arms and waited. I smiled at Stone. His single eye didn't smile.

"Get the bastards."

TWENTY-THREE

THE CLUB CHICAGO was closed, but the doors were open, cleaning women at work inside. The owner was adding receipts at the bar.

"If it's Norma, I ain't seen or heard from her. If it's J.C., she don't come in till six to eat."

"Where can I find her? J.C.?"

He put a rubber band around his receipts. "You said who you were. You didn't show me."

I showed him.

"She's at the Holiday Inn down on the beach. Room twenty-seven."

The Ventura Holiday Inn is a tall, multistory building with a revolving restaurant on top that has a sweeping view of the sea below. I found the house phones near the front desk. Room 27 took six rings to answer, but J.C. Connors didn't sound sleepy.

"Paul Shaw," I said. "Sorry if I woke you up."

"What do you want, Mr. Shaw?"

Early afternoon and not sleepy, but there was something thick in her voice and I didn't think it was too much lunch.

"I want the rest of the story, J.C."

Silence and the clink of something in glass. "What story?"

"The real story," I said. "Whatever's making you drink. The reason you've been watching Norma Powell instead of asking her about Doreen."

The silence became so long I almost wondered if she'd left the receiver off the hook and gone. Almost, but not quite. I heard the faint click of ice against glass.

"The door's open," she said.

I took the elevator to the second floor. Room 27 was on the right, door open. I closed the door behind me. J.C. Connors stood at the wide window that overlooked the sea. She neither turned nor spoke, sipped at the drink in her hand. I stood beside her, looked at the endless view.

"Something made you wait almost a year before coming out to look for Doreen. She's your only daughter, you blame yourself for her running away, yet you waited a year to look for her. That sounds wrong to me, unless there wasn't any particular hurry. Unless there was nothing you could do to help her, and someone else was investigating what had happened."

She drained her glass, left the window, and crossed the room to where the bottle of bourbon and the ice bucket stood on a table. She poured the whiskey over ice, filled the glass at the bathroom sink, returned to the window beside me. Her voice had something of the low, throaty blues sound of her singing.

"They found Doreen at the bottom of a cliff in the Angeles National Forest two weeks after she wrote the last letter." She drank half of her new drink. "She'd been dead at least a week. Too long for them to be sure of exactly the hour or day she died." She drank the rest of the drink. "Lying out there at the bottom of a cliff all alone while I sang for rich drunks in New York. While I boozed, bounced in bed, slept like a baby."

She rotated the ice in her glass. Rapidly. A hard, harsh ringing, the cubes almost unmelted. She looked out at the ponderous sea, then walked again to the table, poured the bourbon, filled the glass in the bathroom, came back.

"I flew out. The police told me it looked like an accident, or suicide, or perhaps both."

"Both?"

She drank. "Her car was parked near where she had fallen, but over ten feet from the edge. She would have to have walked or been carried to the edge. She was full of barbiturates. They said she would have been just about out on her feet, but there was no sign of anyone else being at the top of the cliff. No marks of another car. No evidence of anyone else being in her car, and her car keys were in her pocket." She drank. "They had two theories: She drove up there to kill herself and did; or went up to look at the view and was so stoned she fell over." She swirled the ice in her drink, stared out at the ocean. "They found part of a torn shirtsleeve near the bottom of the cliff. Freshly torn, not out there long. I told them Doreen had never been on drugs. Never! Booze, yes, like mama like daughter, but never drugs. They admitted the newly torn shirtsleeve was suspicious, so decided to investigate. I waited almost a year, but they came up with nothing. No witnesses, no clues, no motive. No one even connected to her except some punkers with alibis. They couldn't find Jack, or the new man, or what she'd been doing that year."

"The four spree kids didn't tell them?"

"They didn't know Doreen had any connection to those four. No one did. There was no address on her. All I had was the box number, and she still had her New York driver's license. That's how they got to me. No one knew where she'd been living, or who she knew. She had no other identification. Her car was the car she'd driven out from New York. No one knew about the four until I found Norma Powell. They talked to them then, but—"

"Talked to them when?"

"About a month ago."

"To Robert Asher, too?"

"I suppose so."

That could have been when Robert Asher became nervous, started to think about hiring a private investigator.

She drank. "The police wouldn't tell me anything about the four, or let me talk to them, probably because of the trial, so I had to find them myself. All the cops told me was that all four said that Doreen had moved away before the drug deal, and that they didn't know where she had gone."

"What about Jack?"

"They've never been able to track him down. I mean, what do they have to go on? I never knew where he lived, what he looked like, or what he did." She drank again, looked into her empty glass. "I haven't done any better. I found Norma Powell. She led me to the rooming house. You got me to the other two in Hermosa Beach. They all say they don't know anything about Doreen, I can't find Jack, and now I've lost Norma."

I could have told her I would find Norma Powell for her. But there are some people who don't need hollow comfort. J.C. Connors would handle it her own way.

"I'll keep in touch."

Outside in the silent motel corridor, I heard her pour another drink, start to sing some low blues song. For her daughter and for herself.

TWENTY-FOUR

A THIN THREAD of smoke stood like a crack in the blue sky beyond the highest peaks of the mountains that ringed Santa Barbara. I watched it, almost mesmerized, the fires beginning to appear everywhere I looked like some kind of ancient plague. At the Union Oil station in Montecito's Coast Village, I got directions to the Walter Maxwell Hardin estate.

The two-lane road took me away from the freeway and the sea up into the dry brown mountains that dominate the narrow coastal plain below. I could almost touch the heat that seemed to come out of the thick bush and dusty oaks. The road wound between high walls and iron gates emblazoned with exotic names that came out of the land of Oz.

The Hardin estate was Monte Oro.

Surrounded by a ten-foot-high wall that extended as far as I could see in both directions, its entrance was a pillared iron gate topped by a grillwork arch with a giant *H* in the center, *Monte* on one side, and *Oro* on the other. A thick forest of eucalyptus, native live oak, palms, pines and trees I couldn't name was massed on the other side of the wall, with no sign of house, lawn or life. I parked, approached the gate. There was no visible lock, but it was firmly closed. An electronic gate. I found the button on the wall itself, a small speaker set into the wall beside it.

"Yes?" a formal voice intoned from the speaker.

"I'd like to see Mr. Walter Maxwell Hardin."

"Whom shall I say?"

"Paul Shaw."

"Thank you, Mr. Shaw."

I leaned against the wall in the sun and surveyed the main road bordered by its rows of blue-gum eucalyptus. Houses covered the fields and slopes among the trees. There was a firehouse up the road, and the low buildings and open playing fields of a school. Children played and cars passed. I felt as if I were at the gates of a feudal castle looking back at the village. A chateau of some French aristocrat before the revolution, the huts of the *Jaquerie* huddled outside.

"Mr. Shaw?" the disembodied voice from the wall said. "When the gates open, drive straight on until you reach the main house. Continue on and park in front of the garages. There will be a side door open in the house. Enter there."

There was a click, and the gates swung silently open. I drove up the gravel drive and heard the ponderous gates close behind me. The private forest could have been on another planet or in another time. Nothing of the outside or even of today seemed to penetrate. Until the drive finally opened onto a vast lawn that sloped down from the house to the trees.

A massive Italianate house that must have been a copy of some Renaissance villa in the Tuscan hills, or the remote estate of a Sicilian prince. In rose-colored stone, it stood two stories high with a flat tiled roof and a tall campanile. A broad stone terrace with terra-cotta balustrade led to wide stone steps that descended through tiers of ponds and gardens until they reached the drive and the great sweep of lawn all the way to the forest that shut out the rest of the world.

The garages were around the mammoth house to the rear, on a level with the first floor. There were an even dozen doorways in the garages, apartments above for the chauffeurs. Off to my left through some tall cypresses, I saw the first tee of a private golf course, and beyond the garages the stables and a full-size polo field. Relics of a bygone age. The Hardins of today didn't build private castles and playing fields; they spread out all across the world and bought the castles and fields they needed.

A side door was open under a giant bougainvillea. Inside, I found myself in a long hallway like a tunnel with light at the far end. Closed doors lined the hallway. Quarters for the more vital servants, so they would be near in case of immediate need. There was a silence in the dim corridor. It was a silence that seemed to have been there a long time. Today even a Walter Maxwell Hardin can't afford the army of people who served his father. Cheap labor is gone, or it was. Lately it's been looking as if it might come back. There's always hope.

As I moved ahead, the dusty silence was like the interior of an Egyptian tomb. Until I reached an enormous kitchen the size of my whole penthouse back on Central Park South. Bright and airy and sunny and as empty as the hallway I'd just left. I began to wonder if anyone really lived in the pink palazzo. Perhaps the voice on the speaker was only a recording left behind when all the living had vanished.

"Mr. Shaw? If you will follow me?"

He stood in a doorway on the far side of the mammoth kitchen. A short, balding, long-nosed, wrinkled old man in gray striped trousers and a black coat. He carried a large silver tray with a silver coffeepot, sugar and cream service, and cups. I followed him into a wide marble corridor out to a front rotunda with the dimensions and marble of a Roman palace.

There were statues, and pools with fountains, and niches with giant colored vases and urns. We crossed into another broad marble corridor that reminded me more of Grand Central Station than the hallway of a house. The butler opened a door and bowed me into a room that seemed to be in the wrong building. Small and lined with walls of books, it had a comfortable-looking leather couch and easy chairs, a desk, and a television set.

"Mr. Hardin will speak with you here," the butler said. "Do you prefer your coffee black or with cream and sugar?"

"Cream and sugar, please."

The butler poured a single cup, added cream and one cube of sugar. He looked at me. I smiled. He put in a second cube, carried the coffee to the desk opposite the televison.

"If you would sit here, Mr. Shaw."

I sat at the desk. The butler turned on the television set, left the room, closed the door behind him.

"You've decided to take my offer, Mr. Shaw?" Walter Maxwell Hardin said.

He watched me from the television set. I stared. Hardin seemed to be in a similar room, with similar furniture and what looked like a swimming pool beyond an open sliding glass door wherever he was.

"Well, speak up. I don't have all day to waste on this."

"I've come to ask some questions," I said. Now I saw the TV camera set into a recess in the wall directly behind the set, aimed at where I sat. The microphone had to be hidden in the desk. A closed-circuit two-way setup. "Where are you?"

"Is that one of the questions?"

"No," I said. "Why are you trying to whitewash Norma Powell?"

"I'm not."

"I think you are," I said. There was something eerie about sitting in a room talking to a television set, a cup of coffee in my hand. "I think you paid Murray Engberg to print those articles about the four dropouts that make Norma Powell look like an innocent dupe, make Robert Asher appear to be the ringleader who led her astray. I think you want to sweep the whole affair out of sight for some reason."

"I don't care what you think, Mr. Shaw."

"Murray Engberg tried to kill me last night."

"Did he?"

"He killed himself instead."

"Unfortunate for him."

"What do you know about Doreen Connors?"

"Never heard the name." He leaned forward on the screen. "Mr. Shaw, I make you the offer once again. A solid offer. Twenty-five thousand to go home and forget about Asher and the others. Yes or no?"

"Why are you so concerned about a two-bit illegal drug bust? They won't get more than five years at most. The closed-down clinics are all open again. The money involved has to be peanuts to you."

"Call it a private matter, Mr. Shaw. Say I'm doing a favor for a friend. Call it anything you like, but go home. Twenty-five thousand."

"A favor for one of their parents? Politics? Some—"

"I don't indulge in politics. I learned long ago it was an unpredictable and totally unnecessary game. Ask your friend Mr. Stone."

Was it a threat? Aware I knew what had happened to Duncan Stone?

"Twenty-five thousand. That's my final offer. After this I'll have to resort to other methods."

"Maybe you already have. You own a couple of chemical businesses, don't you? Pharmaceutical manufacturers?"

"Go home, Mr. Shaw."

The television went dark. The camera on the wall went off. The butler came in.

"Would you care for another cup of coffee before you leave, Mr. Shaw?"

I finished what I had. It was good coffee. Very good. I finished the second cup before I left.

TWENTY-FIVE

I LOOKED UP the steep hill at 947 Valley Road. It was a large Spanish house that shimmered in the heat, with a rolling lawn and wooded grounds of at least two acres. A mansion, if I hadn't just come from the Monte Oro of Walter Maxwell Hardin. A Cadillac was parked in the driveway in front of a three-car garage, and a Latino gardener worked around the red-tile-roofed house. A warmer house, more human, despite its size and grounds, than the vast museum that was Hardin's marble palace.

The woman who opened the door was small, dark, nervous, and dressed in white, drying her hands on an apron. The cook-maid.

"You want?"

"Is Mr. Powell home?"

"I see. You are?"

"Paul Shaw. It's about his daughter, Norma."

I looked across the lawn as I waited. There were trees—oak and palm and red eucalyptus—and other houses were visible through them. A good neighborhood, comfortable and responsible.

"You come."

I followed the Latino cook-maid through a two-story-high entry hall of white walls, dark wood, tiled floor, and hanging tapestries of medieval Spanish scenes. There was an open gallery on the second-floor level as if the high entryway were an inner courtyard. The maid went on along a side hall lined with high-backed wooden chairs like thrones, to an open, glass-walled atrium at the far end. Norma Powell sat in the atrium.

"Why do you want to talk to my father, Mr. Shaw?"

"Mostly to ask about you."

"What is there about me to interest anyone?" She gave a tiny shrug. "Just a stupid girl who needed a boyfriend too much, rejected her parents' world but had to belong *somewhere*. If only to a gang of self-indulgent dropouts."

She didn't ask me to sit down, and she was somehow different and yet not different. Instead of the jeans and T-shirt, hair pulled back by a rubber band, she wore a brown tweed skirt, long-sleeved pale yellow blouse that disguised her full breasts, socks and loafers, her blond hair brushed and curled under. The picture of an Ivy League girl. The face less shy and the body less bold. Older than in the cottage, a twenty-two-year-old upper-middle-class girl, not a teenage waitress. But the voice was as soft, the eyes as large.

"Asher took you into the gang?"

She nodded. "Unstable, Robbie, but somehow dazzling. I should have known better. I'd been raised to know better."

She seemed to be solidly back in her parents' world. That wasn't unusual. The harsh realities of crime and life on the move, wild times hand to mouth, bring a lot of rebellious kids back home where it's safer and warmer.

"How unstable?"

"Violent emotional swings, sudden unpredictable actions. I'm not surprised he's dead. Saddened, but not a lot. Not yet. I don't think it's really sunk in yet. That he's dead, gone."

"Somehow I didn't get that impression of Asher from his widow."

She nodded. "He could have changed, I suppose: I think we all did after it went wrong, came down to earth."

"Your description sounds more like Eliot Drake."

"Yes, Eliot, too. Even Brownlee in his own way. All unpredictable." She thought. "I guess Eliot didn't come down to earth all that much."

"No, he didn't," I said. "Where does a gunman named Jay Norca fit in, Norma?"

"Who?"

I told her about Jay Norca and his visit to her cottage in Ventura. About the beating of the Hartmanns and the "accident" in Hermosa Beach. She seemed to think, smoothed her prim tweed skirt over her thighs.

"He doesn't bring anything to mind, Mr. Shaw."

"Then why did you clear out of that cottage so fast? Walk out on the Club Chicago and Barney?"

"Tired of it. The martyr act, the breast-beating guilt. Tired of that clown of an owner, I suppose. Besides, you were going to blow my cover anyway, right?"

"If he was a clown, why take up with him?"

She laughed. "To see if I could do it. The best man around there, and I needed some man, right?"

It didn't fit her demure Ivy League image, but something in her had been ready to run off with three boys, and none of us is totally consistent. I've known some prim ladies who had very unprim ideas about men.

"You didn't run out because you were scared of whoever killed Robbie Asher?"

"I'm sure that has nothing to do with me."

"And you don't have any idea who Jay Norca was, weren't worried about him."

"No. Should I have been?"

"I'm not sure." I still stood; she still sat with her knees together, her large eyes watching my face steadily. "How about Doreen Connors? Any ideas about what happened to her?"

She shook her head again, slowly this time, sad and almost wondering. "The police came to talk to me over a month ago. I don't know what happened to her or when or why. I couldn't believe it when they told me. The last time I saw her she was so alive, so... What a terrible thing."

"She just moved away a week before the big drug scam."

"Yes. We all helped her. Then we were arrested and we didn't want to get her in trouble, so we never contacted her."

"She had nothing to do with the plan?"

"Just panting after Eliot Drake."

"But Drake had you, so she left."

"Who told you that?"

"Drake."

She laughed aloud. "The dreamer! We played a little, but nothing big. Doreen could have had her share."

"Then why did she leave so suddenly?"

"I don't know why she left or how sudden it was. I wasn't that interested in her. Probably she found a better pair of pants than Drake, at least one she could hope to pin down. Eliot isn't exactly reliable. Perhaps she got wind of our plans and was scared. Perhaps she just got stoned and saw a vision. Ask Drake. He should know more about why she left."

"What do you know about her former boyfriend, Jack?"

"I didn't even know she had one. Jack who?"

"One name is all I know about him."

"That won't get you very far, will it?" She shrugged. "I really didn't pay all that much attention to her. Just another groupie hanging around Eliot, like Robbie's punker. They came and went. That was one of the things that began to bring me to my senses—all the girls that came around. Anyway, I had other problems."

"Such as?"

"Worrying about their scheme, for one thing."

"The drug-scene was theirs?"

"And a sure disaster."

"But you couldn't stop them."

"Too strong for me then."

I heard the word *then* and sensed she was right; they would not be too strong for her now. She had changed enough for that. They would have still been too strong, especially Eliot Drake, for the girl who was a waitress living in the cottage in Ventura, but not for this girl back in her father's house.

"The police spoke to all of you about Doreen?"

"As far as I know."

"Drake and Brownlee didn't say that they knew Doreen was dead."

"I suppose they forgot."

That I didn't believe. That they had forgotten, or that she thought they had. Some other reason, and if she knew what it was, she wasn't going to tell me.

"Why did you let me find you, Norma? I didn't know you were here."

"I wanted you to know my side, the truth. I saw you didn't believe those articles in *Western Ways*. The articles are exaggerated, but they're basically true."

"That's not quite what I've heard."

"Now you've heard my side. With Robbie dead, I guess there's just Eliot, Hal and me. You'll have to make up your own mind." She looked at her watch. "It's getting late. Do you still want to talk to my father?"

"That depends."

She was puzzled. "On what?"

"On what you can tell me about Walter Maxwell Hardin."

"Who?"

"Walter Maxwell Hardin."

I watched her face the whole time. There was no visible reaction beyond a confused look. She seemed to think hard, but shook her head.

"I'm sorry, I know I never heard that name."

"Then I'd like to meet your father."

"Of course."

She stood up and started for another door in the atrium.

"Could you just send the maid for him?"

She stopped, watched me. "You're afraid I'll warn him?"

"You could."

She nodded. "All right." She leaned through the door. "Adelita? Would you ask Daddy to come to the atrium for a moment if he can?"

She returned to her seat. "Who is Walter Maxwell Hardin, Mr. Shaw?"

"Someone who's interested in the four of you and doesn't seem to want me asking questions."

"Interested in us? Why?"

"That's my question."

The man who entered was short and compact. Brisk. A neat, smooth, well-mannered face with short graying hair and nervous blue eyes. A nervousness he covered with the brisk movements. He wore "at home" clothes: loafers, gray slacks, a double-breasted navy blue blazer, blue striped shirt, and gray tie.

"Daddy, this is Mr. Shaw," Norma introduced us. "He wants to ask you some questions."

"Shaw," he said. His grip was firm, but his hand was damp.

"Mr. Powell," I said. "Do you know Walter Maxwell Hardin?"

"Of course," Powell said. "Everyone knows Hardin."

"Personally?"

"I've met him perhaps twice. Large functions. Charities, that sort of thing. I don't know him as a friend, if that's what you mean."

"Do you do business with him?"

"No."

"No involvement at all."

"No."

He had stood facing me ever since we'd shaken hands. In front of me, listening, answering, but not relaxing and not looking at his daughter. His answers were firm and clear and fast. Almost too fast. As if he knew essentially what I was going to ask. Prepared.

"Why would Hardin be interested in your daughter?"

"He wouldn't be."

He did not ask Norma about Hardin, about anything.

"No reason to do you a favor, Mr. Powell?"

"No."

Norma said, "He couldn't be trying to do something to help me to get some favor out of you, Daddy? I mean, some business favor, or political?"

Now Raymond Powell looked at his daughter. "I don' see anything like that, honey. What could I do for Walter Hardin?"

There was a hint of bitterness deep in Raymond Powell' last sentence. But he covered it again with action, looking back at me, smiling, nodding.

"Is that all you wanted to ask, Mr. Shaw? Anything else I can help with?"

"Or me?" Norma said.

"Maybe later," I said.

They both accompanied me along the elegant corridor to the front door. Together, they had a strong family resemblance, and somehow there didn't seem to be that much difference in their ages. I wondered where Mrs. Powell was.

TWENTY-SIX

THE MORNING WISP of smoke in Malibu had grown into a black shroud blowing in the darkening dusk over the dusty canyons of the coast mountains. On the twilight streets and roads near the hospital, the people went about their business as usual, but their faces were sullen as they looked in and up the canyons, an edge of violence in their eyes. They cursed the small push, the accidental bump they would have smiled at and forgiven on another day.

The hospital itself was already crowded with fire victims from the inland canyons. Dazed homeowners who had stayed too long. Exhausted firefighters. The bruised and battered of falls and car crashes in the escape from the inexorable advance of the flames driven by the hot winds. No one paid any attention to me. The police guard outside Duncan Stone's door recognized me, nodded me in. Stone was still in the bed, still bandaged, but he was sitting up, and the pain in the single visible eye was under control.

"So?"

I told him my adventures of the day, from J.C. Connors and the death of Doreen Connors through the television talk with Walter Maxwell Hardin to the return of Norma Powell to her parental fold. His lone unbandaged eye gleamed.

"It has to be the pills, Paul. I've been thinking about it all day. One of his companies made that overproduction, he used those four dumb kids to sell it for him! Now he has to get them off or they'll blow the whistle on him."

"But it looks like whoever is behind it is trying to get only Norma Powell off."

The eye glared, fierce. "Get some off, kill some. Listen, Paul, the only one who really looks bad in those articles is

Robert Asher. He was the one being thrown to the wolves
The whole guilt was laid on Asher, and now he's dead! Th
ringleader is gone, the others all get off, and Hardin is safe.'

"Where does Jay Norca fit in?"

He shook his head in the bandages, winced. "That
haven't figured yet. Maybe he was Hardin's hired gun."

"Then who killed him and why?" I said. "Why was h
looking for Norma Powell and the other two if Hardin ha
a deal with them?"

He sat in the bed breathing and thinking. "Hardin coul
have double-crossed him. Or he could have double-crosse
Hardin. Or both."

"What about Doreen Connors? She could have kille
herself, or someone could have killed her."

"One of the kids? Norca could have been a friend of Dc
reen's looking for her killer. Maybe he was hired to find he
killer? Maybe Hardin had her killed back then a year agc
and Norca was after him."

It was all possible.

"Tell me about the parents of the four."

He sat there breathing for a time, resting. "What do yo
want to know?"

"Could any of them be friends of Hardin's?"

"Hardin doesn't have friends. Only partners, associates
colleagues, and employees."

"Do the parents fit any of those categories?"

Stone shook his head again, winced again. Habits ar
hard to break. "I checked that out pretty good. Asher ha
only a widowed mother up in the Bay area. She lives on
small income and what two older sons give her, plays bridge
had about enough extra in the bank to send Asher to UCSE
Had absolutely no reason to know Hardin."

He was moving in the bed, agitated, as if going over all hi
investigations again in his mind. Restless.

"Brownlee's father is executive vice president at Mei
cury Productions in Hollywood, worked in the old days fc
Harry Cohn and Zanuck. He was a wheel once, made th

decisions and moved the mountains, but he sits back and gets his pay now. Sort of an elder statesman. As far as I know, Hardin's never been near the movie business, and Zack Brownlee isn't a friend.''

"What about Mrs. Brownlee?"

"Lived most of her life in the East, let Zack play his own game out here. Now they sit around the pool in Palm Springs, trade good books, read all about their sons' failures and divorces. She's a solid homebody, no vices and no jealousy that she ever showed.''

"Drake?"

He had begun to breathe harder, the eye not as bright as it had been. "Right-wing activities down on Balboa Bay. Friends of Nixon, Reagan, and Duke Wayne. Frank Drake built and runs his own chemical equipment manufacturing business. Anne Drake is a Ph.D. from Stanford who spent ten years at a right-wing think tank. They both believe five hundred percent in real free enterprise. But Frank Drake believes a thousand percent in law and order, and they've washed their hands of their wayward boy.''

"What does Raymond Powell do?"

He took longer to answer now, the one fierce eye beginning to cloud. "Everything and nothing. He inherited a publishing company from his grandfather: Powell and Haas. He owns about twenty percent, gets a salary and his dividends as long as he stays away from the office. So he invests, sits on a couple of boards, does a lot of local community work. He's a nice gentleman who gardens, golfs, drinks a little, and backs worthy causes. His wife's about the same. Norma's their only child; they do anything she asks them to do.''

He closed his visible eye again, breathed slowly as the pain came back. He had talked too much, pushed too hard. Or I'd pushed him too hard. I had a job.

"Dunc? Anything else? About Hardin or the parents?''

He lay unmoving, the one eye closed. "No." There was a hesitation. I waited. "If it's parents, it would be Powell or Brownlee. But it isn't. Something else."

I left him motionless in the bed. The human body is a fragile thing. A lot more breakable than we think, and hard to put together again. The spirit is even easier to break, and a lot harder to put back together.

TWENTY-SEVEN

I CALLED MILDRED from the crowded hospital lobby.

"Any luck with Jay Norca?"

"He had a record longer than Thayer's memory. Armed robbery to drug dealing. In recent years worked with the same partner every time. The partner has a record you won't believe. He's up in Folsom right now."

"What's his name?"

"Jack Pointer."

"Where was his home base?"

"Los Angeles, according to his last three arrests."

Sometimes it happens just like that.

"Does Dick have a contact up in Folsom?"

"We know the warden, a lot of prisoners."

"See if you can get me a meeting with Pointer."

"It's late now, and it may take a while."

"Try for tomorrow afternoon."

I drove through the night. Flames licked down the slopes of the Santa Monica Mountains, I was hot and tired, and the case would keep until tomorrow. The hot wind swept ashes across the road as I turned into the Hollywood Freeway and then off and up toward Sandra Peterson's apartment.

At her door I had a clear view of the fire spreading across the Santa Monicas, but no answer. Her car was gone. I drove back down and across to Santa Monica Boulevard and Oki Dog. She was there at a table among her Mohawked and dyed, black-leathered and chained, shaved and booted friends. She didn't seem overjoyed to see me, sat and drank her beer and listened to her friends.

"Can I talk to you?"

"Sure."

She didn't move to get up or make room. Her friends watched me like hostile warriors. Dressed in black tights, heavy boots, and a sweat-stained gray sweatshirt with pouch pockets, the dyed and spiked punk wig on, she held her beer in both hands.

"Private."

"Later."

It wasn't me. Or not just me.

"Something wrong, Sandra?"

"Everything." She turned, looked up. "Everything's wrong. I just want to sit and have a beer with my friends. That's all I want to do right now."

"And Robbie? Is Robbie wrong too?"

"Robbie's dead."

"And we have to talk about who killed him."

She sat as if I'd taken all the kick out of the beer. I probably had. Death takes the kick out of most things. Then she stood up and walked ahead of me to my car and got in. I drove back into the hills and up to her apartment perched on its steep slope. She didn't get out, sat with her hands in the pockets of her sweatshirt.

"What's bothering you, Sandra?"

"I told you, everything."

"Me?"

"You, me, Robbie, people who kill people, people who start fires because they live where they shouldn't and don't give a damn about anyone else." She was looking away from me in the dark front seat, out at the night and her front door.

"What bothers you about me?"

Her head turned. All I could see in the dark car was the shine of her eyes, her teeth as she talked. "I like you. How much do you like me? You're married. That's okay. What are you going to want from me? What will you want me to do, want me to be? If I like you, what is it going to make me?"

"I am married. I do live in New York," I said. "Maybe I won't want you to be anything except what you are, what you want to be."

"I like my friends. I feel safe with them. No one's going to tell me what I have to do." She leaned and kissed me. Sat back and stared straight ahead out through the windshield into the night at the single light of a street lamp, the lights in the windows of other houses. "Life is crazy, isn't it?"

"Ridiculous and absurd, but it's all we have."

"Robbie doesn't. Someone took it away from Robbie."

"Is that part of it? Guilt. You and me? Robbie dead?"

"I guess so."

She turned away again. To look out at her high hill and her dark front door.

I said, "Doreen Connors has been dead a year. You had to know that, but you didn't tell me. Why?"

She didn't turn. "God, is everybody dead?" She turned her head, shadowed. "Knew? How could I have known?"

"If not from back then when it happened, you had to know when the police came around to talk to Robbie about her a month ago."

"The police told Robbie Doreen was dead?"

"You knew Doreen before she went to that rooming house and met the four master criminals, and she introduced you to Robbie. Why would she kill herself, Sandra? Or why would someone kill her? Who?"

"I don't know anything about Doreen! Or what troubles she had, or who would kill her! I didn't know she was dead, and neither did Robbie!" She stopped, seemed to be staring at my face, though I couldn't see her eyes in the dark front seat. "At least, not until maybe recently. A month ago? When the police told him Doreen was dead? Maybe that's what changed him, scared him."

It was as possible as anything, if she was telling me the truth. Or if Robert Asher had told her the truth.

"I think I've identified her boyfriend. His name's Jack Pointer. He's serving time up in Folsom right now. He was that gunman Jay Norca's partner. You have any idea where they fit into the picture? Did Asher ever mention them?"

"No. He's a criminal?"

"Looks like it."

"Then . . . maybe he killed Doreen."

"Did Doreen ever say anything that could explain why?"

"She was always scared of him."

"But she'd gone back to him."

She shook her head in the shadows of the car. "I don't know."

She seemed closer than she was in the dark of the car. I could feel her body, the heat of her, the soft flesh and the warmth, the wet inside her.

"You want to go in?"

Her heat and the shine of her eyes.

"No. Yes." The shine vanished, her head turned. "I don't know."

"It's all right."

"I want you, but . . . not now. Not tonight."

"I'm tired anyway."

"I want to go back to Oki Dog."

"All right."

"Please? Just tonight."

"Okay."

"I'm sorry, Paul."

I started the car, drove back down the dark, winding road in the hot night wind from the canyons. Past where Murray Engberg had tried to kill me and died for it. Died to hold onto his job. For a few thousand easy dollars.

"I just want to be out of it all tonight. The whole world."

On Santa Monica Boulevard I turned into the flow of traffic that seemed to move irritably in the heat, with the flames of the distant fire clear against the black hills ahead.

"They're real, Paul. Honest. They have real values, no matter how crazy they seem."

I left her on the sidewalk with the tables and crowded serving windows of the hot-dog stand behind her. She stood and looked after me for a moment. Then I saw her turn and blend into the welcoming punkers.

I drove to the freeway through the ashes and the odor of smoke carried on the hot wind. I could do some work on the case after all.

TWENTY-EIGHT

THE COOL OF the sea came to meet me in the late night. In Hermosa Beach the fires seemed like a distant mirage. No one stood out in the streets watching the sky. Drake's Jensen-Healey was parked in the alley. At the top of the outside stairs the apartment was a blaze of lights and noise. I went up.

A small, slim, red-headed woman answered the door. She looked me over all the way, raised her face, and closed her eyes. I looked her over. A girl. Tiny, in jeans so tight they needed zippers at the ankles, a thin T-shirt over her full breasts, cream-colored cowboy boots so small and high-heeled they made her arched foot seem like the bound foot on an ancient Chinese woman.

She opened her eyes. "Hi."

"Hi," I said.

She seemed to have forgotten she'd closed her eyes, raised her face to me. She seemed to have forgotten me.

"You want something?" She smiled expectantly. "Hey, I know you from somewhere, right?"

"From before you closed your eyes," I said.

"Yeah?" She cocked her head as if I had just told her where we'd met but she wasn't sure I was telling the truth. Her eyes glazed, and then she brightened. "Hi."

"Hi," I said.

"You want something?"

"Drake or Brownlee?"

"What?" She frowned. She looked me over. Her eyes brightened.

I bent and kissed her. I wasn't going to go around the circle again. Her waist was small enough to hold in my hand,

and her retention time was smaller. She opened her lips against mine, flicked her tongue. When she started to climb my legs, I let her go and slid past into the apartment.

"Hey-y-y-y, it's the detective!"

Hal Brownlee lay on the couch someone had covered with a blanket to hide the holes or dirt or both. From the number of legs I could see he wasn't alone. He lay half on top of another slim girl in jeans and a sweatshirt. She was between him and the couch back, and her legs, one shoulder, and some long dark hair in a ponytail were all I could see. That much and her voice.

"Who the hell's he?"

"Detective," Brownlee said. "After all of us because somebody killed Robbie Asher. Poor Robbie."

"Who's Robbie?" the girl said.

"Friend. Robbie was a friend. Good friend, Robbie."

"Who killed your friend?"

"Shhhhhhhhh. Detective's listening."

"He gonna kill you?"

"Who?"

"Guy who killed your friend Robbie."

"I don't know who killed Robbie."

"How come?"

"No one told me."

"Good."

"Why?"

"You don't know him, he can't kill you."

Her voice was triumphant. There were no bottles I could see, but the pungent odor of marijuana hung over the apartment, and beer cans had joined the fast-food litter on the floor. I felt the probing fingers of the redheaded girl on my neck, on my back, under my belt.

"Hey," she said softly, purring into my shoulder blade, tiptoe in the tiny cowboy boots.

"Not interested," Brownlee said from the couch. "He's a detective."

"Cops're interested," the redhead said. "Sometimes." Her face rubbed my backbone. "Hey."

It had to be more than beer or marijuana or even both, for the two women. Probably a combination. I untangled my back from the probing fingers and the body of the little redhead, walked to Brownlee on the couch. Eliot Drake came out of a bedroom.

"Cassie likes you, Shaw." He leaned against the door-jamb. He wore only a pair of blue jockey shorts. He smiled, but I didn't believe the smile. The redhead would be his, and he wasn't someone who shared what was his, or gave it up until he was ready. The redhead, Cassie, would pay later for liking me.

"You didn't tell me Doreen Connors was dead."

The woman half under Brownlee on the couch said, "Who's Doreen Connors?"

Brownlee said, "Old friend. She's dead."

The woman said, "You got weird friends."

"Who says Doreen's dead?" Drake said. He hadn't moved from the bedroom doorway, posed in his skivvies to show his lean muscles. He had a good body. That pleased him.

"The police," I said. "Her mother."

"So I guess she's dead."

I felt the little redhead, Cassie, behind me again. Her light fingers up and down my spine. Her breasts rubbing slowly. Her lips just able to reach my neck. Small teeth biting.

"You didn't tell me."

"It would have spoiled your fun."

"You're always thinking of other people."

He smiled. The "bad" image pleased him too. Bad Eliot Drake. The little redhead was almost hanging off my back, her pelvis and belly pressing rhythmically against my buttocks.

"Maybe," I said, "you knew she was dead long before the police came around last month."

He smiled some more. "Now, how would we have known that? The good gendarmes laid it on us she was all alone out in the big bad hills, stoned out of her G-string. A swan dive. Maybe she thought she could fly. The Icarus bit. The lone eagle out in the boonies on her own. Flew the coop, deserted the troops, bailed out, abandoned the ship. Oh shame, oh remorse, out there to run on her sword."

The redhead was crawling up my back almost to my neck. Whatever she was on was powerful stuff, and whatever they were all on Eliot Drake wasn't. That would be his style. Let them all get high and watch. Use them. Toys for his pleasure. I reached behind me and took the little redhead's wrist, pulled her around in front of me. Her face was up, her teeth biting her lips, her eyes waiting to be stripped, taken.

"Hi."

I led her by the wrist to Drake in his doorway. I put her hands on his shoulders, went back to where I'd been standing near Brownlee and his woman on the couch. They had forgotten I was there. The woman had her pants off and was working on his. By the time I got back to my post the redhead was already climbing Drake's flank, licking at his bare chest.

"She bother you, Shaw?" he said.

"Another time, another place."

The redhead's hands were inside his blue jockey shorts. His smile was thin now, a little tight.

"We bother you, Shaw? I'll bet you're a liberal, a lover of your fellow man. Are we worth it, Shaw? The people you want to save, make the world a better place for?"

"Some of you."

"Shit. None of us is worth saving for ten minutes. A ridiculous tribe of apes on a transient piece of rock in the center of nothing. Absurd and ridiculous. Admit it."

"You're that scared?"

The redhead had his shorts off. Fully dressed in her tight jeans, boots, T-shirt against his naked body. On the couch Brownlee and his woman had their pants off by now, but they had forgotten why. She smoked a joint, lay watching a crack on the ceiling. He sucked a can of beer and played with himself. Sometimes I do wonder if we're worth fighting for, any of us. If we are worth the struggle, or ever will be.

"My eyes are that open!"

It was his weak spot. He could only face death by sneering at it, making it unimportant.

"You and Norma Powell," I said.

"Fuck Norma!"

"She says you're a dreamer, Drake. If you say it was you and her."

The woman on the couch said, "You got any live friends?"

Hal Brownlee nodded vigorously. "Sure. I got you."

The woman thought about that. "Oh, yeah."

"Sweet dreams for her," Drake said.

"That's not what she says. A couple of rolls in the hay and no big deal."

His smile came back. "Why not? Old Norma always did know how to have fun."

The redhead was up to his ear with her teeth, and his cock showed interest at last. For some reason he was feeling better. Picked up the redhead and vanished into the bedroom. He even kicked the door closed. Middle-class training hangs on. On the couch Hal Brownlee and the pair of naked legs half under him were discussing the bright colors on the pale gray ceiling.

The flames in the Santa Monica Mountains guided me all the way back to our hotel. A spreading glow far off across the San Fernando Valley, and a finger of brightness up toward Malibu. I felt like Cortés in the Valley of Volcanoes, ringed by fire.

TWENTY-NINE

THE SUN LIKE a blood-stained orange, and Mildred's cheerful voice on the telephone with bad news, greeted me on the new day.

"Jack Pointer won't talk to you. His exact words, and I quote were 'Tell the cocksucker I eat private eyes and go fuck himself.' What do you want to do?"

"There was a bunco man Dick and I helped beat a murder charge. Emil something. I think he's in Folsom."

"Emil Soto. You proved he was guilty of nothing more than fraud, got him off with two to five. You want me to get through to him?"

"Call me back."

"The instant," she said. "And the new *Western Ways* is out. I'll send it over."

I had time for a shower, probably not breakfast. Emil Soto would be plugged into the prison grapevine, could get word to Jack Pointer faster than the warden or even the governor. He was up for parole soon, he owed me, and the one thing a smart con never forgets is who he owes. There's always a next time. The telephone rang before I was dressed.

"Emil says he'd be honored."

I caught a jet for Sacramento, ate breakfast on the plane, read the latest installment in the *Western Ways* saga of the four dropouts. Once again it hammered away on the theme of Norma Powell as the innocent dupe of the wild, antisocial boys. Norma had only gone along with the schemes reluctantly, without the strength to oppose her man, afraid to lose him. The same message no matter which way you turned it, but the Svengali, the leader, had changed.

It wasn't Robert Asher who had led poor duped Norma down the primrose path of crime. It was Eliot Drake. Drake had been the leader, the instigator, the planner. The change wasn't even subtle. Almost blatant. Eliot Drake was the evil force, with little Norma under his satanic spell. There was no mention of the death of Asher, but I didn't need a crystal ball to know the reason for the shift. A dead man wasn't much good as a scapegoat for a jury to hate.

I rented a car at the Sacramento airport, and two hours later was driving through the foothills of the Sierra Nevadas until the walls of Folsom Prison towered ahead, as formidable as the Great Wall of China. Somber gray granite that seemed to rise in terraces across the whole countryside. A dark growth on the green land.

They admitted me through a stone archway under a squat tower with a pointed roof and a portcullislike gate out of the Middle Ages. There was something medieval about the whole prison, the whole scene and landscape. Savage.

Emil Soto waited in a small visitor's room with only a few other prisoners and visitors on this weekday afternoon. The relatives of convicts don't usually have weekdays free.

"What you gonna do for me this time, Shaw?"

Small and thick in prison gray, the stereotype of a Mexican even to the long, drooping bandit mustache and high Indian cheekbones. Indian cheekbones and a long Castilian nose. Mayan lips and quick American eyes.

"What are you going to do for yourself, Emil?"

He motioned for a cigarette. I gave him one, lit it. The other visitors and cons were deep in whispered conversation. Some of the women were crying, the prisoners comforting them. Some women were swearing. Some men were crying.

"Man," Emil Soto said, "what you want from me? I'm forty years old, I dropped out of a high school had teachers so bad they wouldn't of been let mop floors in no good school. I can just maybe read 'n write in two languages. I got no skills, 'n I can't work for no minimum pay 'n make it with my family. I got to con 'n steal to live. If there was more jobs outside, most of us here wouldn't be in the joint, 'n there wouldn't be near so much crime outside. In here you ain't rehabilitated; you's just kicked 'n punished 'n made to hate the whole fuckin' world you was born into.''

He had a captive audience, and he knew it. He didn't want an argument, but he got one.

"No one has to become a criminal, Emil.''

"What you talkin', man? You know what this here country it wants ever'one they should do? Buy, man, buy ever'-thing they is! They ain't meanin' me, on'y they make a mistake, you know? They gimme lousy schools, stinkin' jobs, 'n a garbage dump to live in, but they gimme a TV set, too, 'n I sees all them shiny ads same as ever'one else. Them big ads with the smilin' white broads—hey, man, buy, live, have fun! They forget they gotta say, 'Not you, José. We don' mean you, *pachuco*. Stand back, nigger.' So we sees them ads 'n we gets the message, 'n we wants to buy all that great stuff too. I mean, our kids, they sees 'n they wants what ever'one else's kids wants. You makes us want it all, then you don' give us no way to get it. If'n we just don' lie down 'n take it, we got two ways to go. We say no, we don't want no part o' your fuckin' world, we gonna change your fuckin' world, 'n that makes us bad-ass cases, troublemak-ers, Commies. We say yes, we wants to smell nice too, we wants to drink the right brew, get all them broads with great teeth, 'n if we got to steal to get it, then we steals.''

"And spend half your life in prison.''

"Half in the joint beats all in shit.''

What answer did I have? Emil Soto didn't really expect one. He knew the answers.

"Okay, Shaw, what you want I should do?''

"I have to talk to a con in here. He doesn't want to talk to me. Can you get him a message?''

"What con?''

"Jack Pointer.''

"Shit! That's heavy, Shaw.''

"A bad one?"

"Mean 'n crazy. I don' like I should mess with that kind."

"All I need is to get the word to him."

"What word?"

"Tell him I'm investigating the deaths of Doreen Connors and Jay Norca. If he helps me with Doreen, I'll help him get Norca's killers."

Soto thought, chewed his mustache. He owed me, and he could see no special danger to him. He held out his hand for another cigarette. I gave him the pack. He nodded, motioned to the guard. After they had left, I went back to the warden's office to wait for a message. The warden was a personal friend of Dick Delaney. It always pays to have influence. Anytime, anywhere. He even had his secretary give me a cup of tea while I waited. It was a short wait.

The telephone rang inside the warden's private office. He came out to tell me Jack Pointer had changed his mind, would see me. He took me along the corridor to a small room with a table and two chairs.

"There'll be a guard watching the whole time. Keep your hands in sight, Mr. Shaw, don't get any closer than across the table, and don't turn your back on Pointer. He's violent and unpredictable. Good luck."

I sat at the empty table to wait. There was something uneasy, even eerie, as I waited alone in the silent room, aware of the thousands of violent men all around me.

THIRTY

THE MAN WHO came into the small room was as cold and grim as the prison itself. Tall and skinny, with long arms and eyes that never stopped moving, searching for what he didn't even know himself. Predator eyes. Almost black in his sallow, stubbled face, seeing the entire room and me in a single glance.

"Who got Jay?"

"I'll find out. If you help me."

His walk was a stiff glide. Short steps, his eyes never off me. Sat across the table.

"Help how?"

"Tell me everything about Doreen Connors."

He sat, watched me.

"It's all part of the same thing," I said.

He waited.

"Whoever killed Norca is mixed up with the four kids."

I told him the whole case except the names of J.C. Connors and Walter Maxwell Hardin. I wasn't going to hand them over to the mercies of Jack Pointer. At least not until I knew more about where they fitted in it all. He held his hand out for a cigarette. All cons cadge; you never know about tomorrow in a prison. I'd come prepared. He lit the cigarette himself, leaned back.

"She shacked with me maybe a year, maybe more, it ain't easy to keep 'em straight. 'Bout a year ago I'm off on a job and she splits. Good riddance. Me and Jay had word on a sweet deal anyway, no time for layin' around dippin' pussy with hot-pants Doreen. A real sweet setup: reds, bluebirds, speed, bennies, rainbows, the works. All we got to do is run a hijack over Arizona and the company made the stuff can't say diddly shit!'' His thin lips skinned back over yellow teeth in what had to be a grin as he remembered how easy it had been. ''Not a fucking thing they could do, 'cause it was all under-the-table overproduction they figured to sell to junk dealers and make a tax-free bundle. We had 'em cold by the *cojones*.''

The memory of his triumph didn't last long. The bared teeth held the cigarette, and it wasn't a grin. ''Then the bitch shows up again. Doreen! Walked in one day after me and Jay got back with the stuff, wanted me to take her back. What the hell, I always liked the kid, I'd have time soon, right, and she said she'd tried to forget me but couldn't make it. So I took her back.'' His eyes, face, everything darkened. He hunched forward, coiled. ''What a royal ass-hole she made out of me!''

His jaw muscles were so tight I thought he'd bite the cigarette in half. ''A week after she comes back, the cops crawl all over me and Jay! Out of bed, hauled in, and sweated 'round the fucking clock! Where are the goddamned pills? We don't tell them, right? Only they find out anyway and we're on the hook.'' He blew smoke as if the stream of smoke would cut a hole in the air, the muscles like ropes in his neck. ''We gets into court a month later and it turns out the cops they finds only half the pills we hijacked, right? The rest was gone before the cops got to where they was stashed. Right then we knows we been ripped off. We been fingered and ripped off both, and it don't take no fucking UN meetin' to figure out who done it, right? That's why she come sneakin' back—to finger us and grab the pills!''

''Not for herself,'' I said. ''For four enterprising college dropouts. Only how did they know about the pills at all?''

''She told 'em, what else? The deal came up before she cut out. She knew we was gonna grab the stuff over in Arizona. All she hadda find out was where we had 'em, and I showed her that myself out on a fuckin' drive in the country!''

He held his fury so tightly his sallow face got paler. Hell has no fury like a woman scorned, and there is no rage in heaven like love to hatred turned. But for real hate and real rage, give me a strong-arm hustler and bully who's been made a fool of.

"So the cops got us, and those kids got half the pills. Only Doreen, she disappears soon as we get picked up, and without her the cops ain't got a real case against Jay. Me, I was spotted over in Arizona. I rented the truck we used. I makes a deal: I take the top fall, Jay gets charges dropped."

"On the outside he can go after Doreen and the kids."

He breathed deeply, inexorably. "Nobody makes a royal asshole out of me and Jay. First he goes after little Doreen. Only someone beat us to her—the cops picked her up dead at the bottom of some cliff."

"Norca didn't kill her?"

He shrugged. "Why'd I lie about it now? I want who got Jay."

"Who did kill her?"

"She was junked to the eyeballs, figured she could walk on air. Maybe she was just so scared we'd get her, the bitch, she saved us the fuckin' trouble."

With Norca dead, Pointer had no reason to cover for him, but he'd lie by reflex anyway. There was no way of being sure, nothing to go on but judgment, an educated guess, fifty-fifty.

"So Jay goes on after them four tight-assed kids figured they was big deals. Turns out they blew the whole fuckin' show! Got collared before they sold a pill, all up for trial. Except they let 'em out on bail. Me and Jay would've rotted, but them they let out and Jay can't find where they are. He been diggin' for 'em ever since, only someone got him first."

Fury, outrage, a certain confusion—who could have killed Jay Norca?—and perhaps a little uneasiness on his gray hawk face.

"I think he got one of them," I said.

His face cheered up. "Yeah?"

"He found Robert Asher and killed him and went on after the girl, Norma Powell. But I'd reached her, told her what had happened to Asher, so she ran and Norca missed her. Then he went for the last two, but someone stopped him before he got to them."

His cigarette was burned down to his fingers. "One of them. It got to be."

I shook my head. "Brownlee and Drake aren't killers. Drake thinks he's bad, but he's a middle-class smart-ass Norca would have had for breakfast. They couldn't kill anyone, not even in self-defense. If Norca showed up around them, they'd run for the cops."

I could almost smell his skin on fire where the cigarette darkened his permanent nicotine stains. "So who you got could of done it?"

"You know a gray-haired man, late sixties, well dressed, rich, has two moose for bodyguards?"

"No." He didn't even notice his skin burning. "He got a name?"

"Not yet."

He only watched me, stared at my face.

"Or," I said, "it could be the same one who killed Doreen."

He finally dropped the tiny butt of his cigarette. "You don't buy she took a dive?"

"Seems like a hell of a coincidence."

Now he rubbed at his cigarette-stained fingers, slowly. "Jay don't get her, who does?"

"That's why I'm here. Anything she said when she came back? Anything she did? Anyone she talked about? Any problems she had, worries?"

He thought. It wasn't something he was used to doing. He even forgot to ask for another cigarette. He shook his head. A year was a long time in Jack Pointer's life.

"Where'd she been the time she was away from you?"

"Hangin' around those punk jerks. Livin' in Santa Monica somewheres." He scowled, concentrated. "That kid you said Jay got. What the hell was his name?"

"Robert Asher."

"Yeah, Asher. I didn't pay no real mind. I mean, who cares who she was playin' with, right? I got my other skirts, too. She come back, what the hell, right?"

"What about Asher?" I said.

"She says once she met this here guy at that hot-dog stand she goes to in Santa Monica was real nice, a real nice guy! Like I wasn't a nice guy, right? Who the fuck wants a broad to say he's a nice guy? Anyway, she says this Asher is a nice guy, she was gettin' tight with him; I don't treat her right, maybe she goes and finds this Asher. I belted her one, told her to go back any fuckin' time she wanted."

"You're sure? Asher?"

"Yeah, Asher. I remember, 'cause I said she wanted some ashes, she could haul mine anytime!"

"Not Drake?"

"Nope, Asher."

I got up. "I'll be in touch."

He watched me all the way to the door. "You find whoever, then you get him sent up here. Get 'em all sent up here, those fuckin' smart kids. Right up here, and they're dead."

I believed him.

The warden passed me out, and I felt a weight lift as I drove under the gray medieval tower and heard the gate close behind with me on the outside. It made me think about the perpetual weight carried day by day, minute by minute, by those who heard the gate close with them on the inside of the cold gray walls. If it happened young enough, long enough, often enough, there was no way the endless weight wouldn't twist them into a dark shape that had no name, that was no longer human.

THIRTY-ONE

IN THE HOLDING pattern, the jet circled over Los Angeles and the valleys. The smoke of the fires in the San Gabriels, the Santa Monica Mountains, Malibu, and Santa Barbara far to the north seemed to ring the world. A firestorm ready to engulf the universe. But there is more than one kind of firestorm, and I thought about Robert Asher and Doreen Connors as we came down into LAX.

It was after 5:00 P.M. when I wound up into the Hollywood Hills with the hot wind blowing the car but doing nothing for the sweat under my shirt. Sandra opened the door before I rang. She wore her real hair, dark and long on her shoulders. A dress tight on her hips, on her whole body. Green. She looked cool and slim even in the heat.

"I was watching for you," she said.

I closed the apartment door. "You don't have to wear a dress for me."

"I want to."

"I like you in jump suits, pants."

"I'm sorry about yesterday."

She had the dinner table laid, even a cloth.

"You were being pushed too fast," I said.

"I guess," she said, looked at the table and its neat place settings for two. Stemmed glasses that didn't match. "I missed you last night."

"Give it some time."

She sat on her couch, knees together in the skirt, perched. "I got a red wine. I mean, I had it. Robbie had it. Robbie liked wine. Especially California reds—the big, heavy ones. I didn't want to stay home last night. Robbie liked to stay home, buy good California reds. Last night I wanted to run, swing in the trees, you know? Tonight I want to sit. Just sit."

"Then let's sit."

Her smile was ten years younger. "It's chicken livers. I make them special. New York style."

Maureen makes them special too. New York style. Does a man always want the same woman? A woman attract the same man?

"With fettucine noodles and asparagus?"

"Salad. How'd you know about the noodles?"

"I like fettucine noodles."

She led me to the table the way a child leads you to its first Christmas tree. She had the wine breathing, the bread warm, the chicken livers ready. Maureen cooks them better, but she was three thousand miles away. The wine was good. A big zinfandel you could bite into. Too big and heavy for the hot night. I had my mind on other things.

"I found Jack."

She ate a liver. "Jack? Oh, Doreen's invisible lover? Where? Who is he?"

"His name's Jack Pointer, he's a professional hoodlum, thief, con artist, strong-arm man, and he's up in Folsom."

"The prison? He's in jail? Then—"

"He couldn't have done anything himself, but Jay Norca, the gunman in the brown suit, was his partner and was tracking down everyone involved in the sale of those pills."

"Tracking? You mean . . . ?"

"I think he killed Asher, yes."

She put down her fork.

"Pointer and Norca hijacked those pills from a pharmaceutical company, and the four dropouts stole them from Pointer and Norca. They used Doreen. Doreen knew about the deal, must have told one of the four, and they decided to turn Pointer and Norca in, steal the pills, and sell them for themselves. They sent Doreen back to find out where the pills were. She did. But got cold feet, wanted out, and someone killed her."

"They stole the pills from two professional criminals?"
I ate my fettucine. "Yeah."

"My God." She drank wine. "Robbie never told me."

"Someone killed Doreen."

She drank again. "Animals!"

"Doreen told Jack Pointer that Asher liked her. If Pointer didn't treat her right, she'd go back to Asher."

I watched her. Ate the chicken livers and fettucine and watched her. She stopped drinking her wine.

"Doreen?"

"That's what Pointer says she told him. Not Drake; Asher. He remembers because he made a joke about her hauling his ashes."

She ate a chicken liver. "You think I killed Doreen."

"You didn't tell me about her and Robbie."

She drank wine. "Jealous and killed her."

"She was probably killed before the deal ever happened. Perhaps not over the pills at all. Not by Pointer or Norca or one of the four."

She ate her chicken livers, drank her wine. Gravy and fettucine. Anger made her eat more and drink more. Angrily.

"You really think I could have killed Doreen."

"Why not tell me Doreen liked Robbie?"

"Because she didn't! Not that I ever saw or Robbie ever said. Not that she ever showed!"

"Then why tell Pointer she did?"

"I don't believe she did."

"He has no reason to lie about it now, Sandra, and every reason not to. He wants Norca's killer caught. The more he can tell me, the better I can work."

Drank. "Then she lied to him."

"Why?"

"To confuse him, make him chase the wrong man if anything went wrong. To protect Drake. She was always stupid over men. If she was swooning for Drake, she'd have protected him, saved her true love."

She finished her wine. Her eyes defied me to contradict her. Angry, yet somehow not at me. As if we had passed a point of interaction and it was all right for me to think she could have murdered out of jealousy if I had a logical reason. But angry at something, perhaps at murder itself.

"If she was swooning for Drake," I said. "And if Drake needed protecting. Perhaps those articles were right in the first place, and Robbie was the leader. Norma Powell says all three of them were, but Brownlee's no leader, so that leaves two."

She refilled her wineglass. And mine. "Robbie wasn't the leader. Drake and Norma were. They were the ones who wanted to turn it all from a rebellion into an attack, beat the world, get money for the 'cause.' Only Robbie started to realize they just wanted money for their own private cause, to get rich. He told me that when Doreen brought him around and I met him. He wanted to break away from them. That was even before it went wrong. Before they tried to sell the pills."

"But he didn't," I said.

"No." She drank the red wine. "And it cost him. It cost him everything there is. Pffft! Gone! It all ends, you know? Ends and changes. I don't want it to change, but it will. It's all horseshit. The whole world."

"He didn't break away, and maybe he didn't tell you everything, or even anything true."

"And they killed him?" She sat in the chair, the wine in her, and forgot she was wearing a dress. Her slim legs spread. A dress without underwear. Naked under the dress. For me. "How do we find out? How do we ever know?"

"We keep walking and keep asking," I said.

"Ask who? They'll all lie."

"Tonight we'll go and ask Drake and Brownlee. They'll lie, but lies don't hide everything. You can tell a lot from lies, from what kind of lies."

In the apartment, close, there was more wine and nothing at all under her dress but the shadows of her thighs and higher. I didn't want to go and ask Drake. But I had to go and ask Drake.

THIRTY-TWO

WITH THE SOUND of the surf close in the night, the fires were far away. But the odor of smoke penetrated even the alley in Hermosa Beach. There was a light in the third-floor rear, but no noise. At the top of the stairs there was no answer to our ringing. As usual, the door wasn't locked.

The dark living room showed all the marks of the party the night before, from beer cans and the strong smell of marijuana, to skewed furniture and pillows on the floor. The light came from one of the bedrooms. Not the one Eliot Drake had carried the clinging redhead into.

"Who is it?"

Shading his eyes, Hal Brownlee lay under the sheets of a sagging iron bed. He sweated in the hot night, looked cold at the same time, the sheets held tight to his chin. His eyes were red and miserable as he tried to see through the light to where Sandra and I stood in the bedroom doorway.

"Whoever it is, go away."

He pulled the sheet up over his face, lay rigid. I walked closer, stood over the bed.

"It's Paul Shaw. Where's Drake?"

"Go away."

I sat on the bed. "Too much fun last night?"

He pulled the sheets down from his face. "How do you know about last night?"

"I was here."

"You were?" He frowned. "I thought it was just Sybil and Cassie. I mean, with Eliot, too. Who'd you bring?"

"I just stopped in to talk."

"You talk to me?"

"I did."

"Christ!" He shook his head on the pillow. "I guess I made out with Syb, too, but I don't remember." He saw Sandra standing behind me. "Who's that?"

"Sandra Peterson." I said.

She stepped closer, stood looking down over my shoulder where I sat on the bed between her and Brownlee. The light was behind her, and he had to shade his eyes again. He went pale.

"That's not her name! Sandra, but not Peterson. I don't remember. Robbie Asher brought her around. Sure! Robbie and Doreen brought her to the rooming house, and..." He remembered. "She married Robbie. Jesus." He shivered under the sheets in the hot night. "Eliot's crazy, you know." Shivered again. "I don't like to be alone. He shouldn't go off like that. He shouldn't leave me here alone."

"Where'd he go?"

He gripped the edge of the sheet in both hands. "I'm scared alone. He knows. They'll find us. I told him all along. I know they'll find us."

"Pointer and Norca?"

"They found Robbie Asher. They'll—" His bloodshot eyes widened and stared past me at Sandra. "They know her! They'll follow her!"

He sat up, shrank against the wall at the head of the iron bed. He was fully clothed under the covers, sat now like a prisoner in a padded cell. I didn't know if it was permanent panic or the hangover of last night's drug-and-beer burnout or a combination of both.

"Norca's dead and Pointer's in prison," I said. "They can't hurt anyone right now. Where did Drake go?"

He huddled against the iron bed and the wall. "He knows I can't stay alone. I can't breathe alone. He knows."

"Where is he, Hal?"

His breathing was labored where he huddled. More than the hangover of last night, but fueled by the hangover. The shakiness that can become fear the morning after. Breathed long and slow, watched me, watched us.

"He's going to get us killed, Mr. Shaw. He's not as tough as he thinks he is."

"Few people are."

"He's got some new scheme to get rich, and he's going to get us killed. The last scheme's got us all going to jail, and now he's got another and we'll get killed."

Sandra said, "Who had the idea to steal those pills?"

"They did. Not me."

"Who're they?" Sandra said.

"Eliot and Norma." His shaky voice grew bitter. "It was always Eliot and Norma. Everything we did. Now he's going to get us killed. Killed just like Robbie Asher!"

"And Doreen," I said.

He nodded, moved closer to us. "We didn't know she was dead. She told Eliot about Pointer and the pills, and he and Norma cooked up the plan. Doreen was scared, but she went through with it. Only after she told us where to get the pills, she was so scared Pointer would find her she wanted out. Eliot and Norma said okay, even helped her move. I never saw her after that. I mean, we were arrested maybe three days later. Just dumb kids, and we still are. At least Doreen was stoned half the time. I remember she was real stoned the last time I saw her."

"When was that, Hal?" I asked.

"The day she moved out."

"When Eliot and Norma helped her move?"

He nodded. "Me and Robbie Asher packed her stuff for her, and Eliot and Norma helped her move wherever she went. Then we all got arrested, and we never knew what happened to her until the police came and told us maybe a month ago. I guess Pointer found her the way she was always afraid he would."

He was half sitting up, seemed almost back to normal.

"Now you're afraid of Drake's new scheme," I said, "whatever it is."

"He won't tell me. Just sits there and laughs and says it's like shooting ducks in a barrel and we're going to be rich after all, maybe not even go to jail."

"And tonight?"

"Said he had to consult with his little partner and left me here alone. I hate being alone." He looked around the barren bedroom, the sound of the surf outside and the smell of distant fires. "He shouldn't go and leave me alone."

I looked back as we left. Brownlee was already back under the sheet pulled up to his chin, staring at the ceiling.

THIRTY-THREE

THE COFFEE SHOP was close to the beach, the white edge of the surf visible in the hot night. In the heat people lay all across the beach itself, cooled in the white foam, or swam farther out. Silent shadows against the white beach, dark ghosts in the surf and smoke-streaked moonlight.

She drank her coffee. "You still think I killed Doreen?"

"I don't know who you killed," I said. "I don't know you. I work in a sad profession in an indifferent world."

She thought and looked through the dirty windows toward the dark ocean. "I suppose I could have. I suppose we all could, under the right circumstances."

"No, we all couldn't."

"You're sure?"

"Brownlee couldn't." I drank my coffee. It was bitter and lukewarm. "Not even to save his life. Someday we may all be like that. Then we'll have a chance."

"Drake could, couldn't he?"

"And Norma Powell."

"And you," she said. "I guess we don't know each other yet, do we?"

Somehow, I liked the "yet." There'd been a lot of other women over the years—part of the territory, part of who I am and who Maureen is. This one was different. Or perhaps it was only that time in my marriage. Or me. Or Maureen. Or both of us and a certain point in our lives. Or perhaps it was Sandra.

I said, "Who do you think Drake's 'little partner' could be?"

"Who knows? His latest lady friend, I suppose."

"You're sure it's a woman?"

She pushed her coffee away. "When a man like Drake calls someone his 'little' anything, it's a woman."

The coffee was now cold and sour.

"And when he uses the word 'partner,' it could mean an unwitting partner, a tool, a victim."

"I suppose," she said. She pulled her coffee back, took a sip. "I don't know what I want, do I? Maybe it's just that I don't really want anything permanent, enclosed. Maybe I never did. Nothing tight, chained. I want somewhere to belong without risk, you know? I don't want any time to stop and think. Not after Robbie. I don't want to think about Robbie and how it ends."

"Can you tell me what you do want?"

"I don't think so," she said. "Except you. In bed. Now."

She started to pick up the coffee mug, a scum of gray milk now floating on its cold surface. Grimaced, pushed it away again, looked sideways out the window to where the people sprawled motionless all over the pale white expanse of the beach at the end of the street, stood like black ghosts against the spume of the surf in the hot night.

"My place is a hotel room," I said. "I don't like hotel rooms."

"We always go to my place," she said. "It's a tradition."

We paid for the coffee, even left a tip. It's easier to keep up the codes, appearances, the proper ritual. Even the euphemisms.

"I have to wash my hands."

"I'll wait in the car."

I walked out into the hot wind and thick heat mixed with the odor of the sea. They were waiting for me.

"Smile and walk to the limo."

They took positions on either side of me. Hardin's musclemen. Fully dressed in suits, ties, white shirts, polished dress shoes, even they looked wet and wilted in the hot Santa Ana night. Irritable, their hands in their suit coat pockets. Not that they would need guns to hold me. I walked between them to the long black limousine. I saw Sandra come out of the coffee shop. She stared toward me. I looked right through her, shook my head an inch.

"In," one of them said.

I stumbled as I got into the limousine, laid my keys on the ground under the big car, looked back toward Sandra. The invisible driver drove away.

THIRTY-FOUR

IT WAS A narrow, blacktopped road that curved up dark slopes through pines and redwoods. We had been driving for hours. Freeways and then back roads. Through San Bernardino and off into the mountains. Neither giant in the shadowed rear of the limousine had said a word since Hermosa Beach. I hoped Sandra had found the car keys. Even gotten the limousine's license plate.

"Left."

The silent limousine took the left fork at a junction high in the pines. It curved through the ghostly trees to an almost hidden massive wooden gate. The gate was open now in the late-night shadows of the mountains, and the narrow road went on another half a mile until the land opened up into a great parklike expanse. In the center of the park, a turreted gray stone mansion with peaked gables and mullioned windows stood high on the downslope of the mountain. The picture of an English country estate, with a sense of dark wood, horses, men in armor.

"Out."

The front door at the top of a flight of narrow stone steps was shaped like the back of an altar, stained glass over it. No one came out of the house. One of the giants opened the door, pushed me inside. The entry hall was like every baronial stage set Broadway or Hollywood ever used. Dark curved wood, maroon velvet hangings, tapestries, broad staircase, swords and shields on the walls. Even the rich have their clichés.

"Inside."

Off the Graustarkian entry hall was a comfortable library with walls of books and high, narrow windows of small panes. There were leather chairs and couches, thick rugs, and a large inlaid desk with Walter Maxwell Hardin behind it.

"Sit down, Mr. Shaw."

I sat down. He held a drink, sat back in the desk chair, watching me. He swirled the drink, the clink of ice the only sound. A Japanese houseman appeared on some hidden signal, offered me a Tadcaster porter on a silver tray. He poured the ale, looked at Hardin. The tycoon smiled, nodded. The house wasn't his; it was clearly loaned, with servants. The rich never pay rent or hotel bills—there is always someone to lend them a house for a week, a month, wherever they want to go.

"I asked you to drop the affair, Mr. Shaw. I told you to go home to your wife, forget about Robert Asher and the others. I'm sorry you didn't."

The porter was as good as ever. Hardin wore a blue pinstriped suit this time, three piece, real cashmere, with gold watch chain and some organization key I didn't recognize. His gray hair was as neat as ever, his tie a red and blue regimental: The Guards. His tan seemed to have faded and he looked a lot older than he had in the Santa Monica pub.

"So you can whitewash Norma Powell, twist the truth, sweep most of it out of sight under your money? Buy articles, delays, public opinion? Corrupt justice?"

"What business of yours is any of that, Mr. Shaw?"

"Robert Asher is my business. What happened? Was Asher going to fight back, spoil your plans? Was that why he was killed?"

He went on slowly swirling his drink, sipping occasionally. A darkish brown drink, with soda from the bubbles. He enjoyed the drink, but his attention was on me.

"I never met Robert Asher. I never knew anything about Robert Asher other than his name and that he had been involved in the juvenile drug-sale scheme. A name, nothing more. Just a name I could use to establish the real truth."

"Your men knew about him, probably met him. One of them anyway."

"Gabe there was checking Asher from time to time, and Harry was watching Drake and Brownlee. Simply keeping track of them for me. Gabe observed you arrive at Asher's apartment, went up to listen."

I looked over my shoulder at the two private Gestapo men who leaned on the paneled walls on either side of the door. Neither of them moved or spoke.

"A contact mike in the briefcase?" I asked Hardin.

"I never ask their methods."

"I hope they're better than Murray Engberg's."

"So do I." He even smiled as he drank. "I don't respect a man who makes a bold move for his advantage but does not face the full consequences. He should have planned what to do if the articles were questioned. Instead he panicked."

"Maybe he guessed there was more to the case than just being paid to print phony articles."

He shook his head. "There is no 'case,' Mr. Shaw. A minor crime by four juveniles a full year ago, and a trial that will be over in half a day. Nothing was actually sold. My lawyers say we'll probably get them off with probation, perhaps a few years at most."

"Funny, somehow I thought I was investigating three murders."

"Three?"

I finished my porter. "Asher and the gunman, Jay Norca—?"

"Jay Norca?"

"One of the two professional criminals those fool kids stole the pills from. The partner went to prison, but Norca got off and went after the four kids. When I ran into him, he was in the Ventura cottage looking for Norma Powell. But she'd skipped out, so he went to Hermosa Beach after Eliot Drake and Hal Brownlee. Only he was killed before he could get to them in an accident that wasn't any accident."

The Japanese appeared again. Hardin handed him his empty glass. Mine was still half-full. The houseman left. Hardin sat and waited quietly, unmoving, except to raise his eyes and look out one of the narrow windows at a single distant light somewhere in the valley far below. The Japanese returned with another dark drink that bubbled with soda.

"Martel?" Hardin said.

"Martel and soda, Mr. Hardin."

Hardin sipped the drink, nodded. The Japanese vanished.

"A professional gunman has nothing to do with us," he said, decided. "From the sound of it, he certainly killed your Robert Asher, and whoever may have killed him did the authorities and the citizens a considerable favor. I see only another mitigating factor for the others—hounded by a professional killer."

I drank my porter and watched him. He thought of everything in terms of what it meant to him. What he could do with whatever it was. How it could be of use to him. Where the advantage lay for him. There had to be some advantage in everything if he looked at it hard enough.

"I wonder what you'll make out of the third murder," I said, finished the porter.

"I've already told you I have no connection to any murders."

"Doreen Connors," I said. "A year ago out in Angeles National Forest."

He was losing patience with me, drank his brandy angrily. "I have never heard of Doreen Connors. My God, the names people give their children! I'm not interested in Doreen Connors. Not everyone who dies in California is my business."

The Japanese materialized with another Taddy porter and a fresh glass. I nodded thanks, poured.

"A year ago the four juveniles, as you call them, met Doreen Connors in the rooming house in Santa Monica. She got close to Eliot Drake or Asher or Norma or maybe all three. She'd run away from a nasty gentleman friend named Jack Pointer. I just came back from visiting Pointer up in Folsom Prison."

"Did you?"

He drained his brandy. The Japanese appeared on cue with a fresh drink. Hardin didn't even look at him, too busy looking at me. A faint flicker of the dark Oriental eyes made me think the houseman wasn't that happy at being on loan to Hardin. Not that that would bother Hardin or the owner of the house. To the rich, the furnishings, animate or in-animate, went with the house.

"You want to know what I learned at Folsom?"

"Tell me."

I drank. My throat was getting drier and the black ale slid down thickly. "It seems Pointer and Norca planned a hi-jacking Doreen knew all about. Doreen told Drake or Asher or Norma about what Pointer and Norca were doing. The four eager dropouts cooked up the scheme to steal the loot— a truckload of pharmaceutical overproduction—and turn Pointer and Norca in to the police to get rid of them. As crazy and dangerous a scheme as anyone could think up, but they went through with it."

"A stupid scheme," Hardin said, nodded, "but one I al-ready knew all about, Mr. Shaw."

"And Doreen Connors?" I said. Was I talking my way out of trouble or into it? My throat was getting drier even with the thick porter going down. "She was the connection to the pills, and she fingered Pointer and Norca so they could get at the pills. She supposedly got cold feet, was scared to death, and moved out before the scam went down. A week later she was found dead in the Angeles National Forest with no identification except out-of-state. No one connected her to our four dropouts until a month or so ago."

He was frowning into his brandy as if he suspected the houseman of putting something over on him, using inferior brandy or domestic sparkling water. Sometimes I feel sorry for the very rich. Like beautiful women, they're always afraid someone is trying to take advantage of them.

"What is your point, Mr. Shaw?"

"Someone killed Doreen Connors almost a year ago."

"Undoubtedly your criminals, Pointer and Norca."

"Pointer was in jail. I think Norca killed Robert Asher, but I think Doreen Connors was dead before Norca found her. I think she was dead before the drug deal took place. Someone else killed her, and someone killed Norca in Hermosa Beach."

He nodded. "I had hoped you could be persuaded even now to go away. I'm sorry." He stood up. "I don't know who killed your Doreen Connors, or why, but I had to stop Norca. He was a murderer, a thief, pure scum. He had killed Asher, was a danger to the others."

The two musclemen seemed to come alert at the door behind me. Hardin had just confessed to murder. And he hadn't broken Jay Norca's neck himself.

"Your 'assistants' could have done a better job."

"We were in a hurry," Hardin said. "There was no time for proper planning."

"Life can be like that," I said. "When did you fall in love with Norma Powell, Mr. Hardin?"

THIRTY-FIVE

I IMAGINED I could hear the wind blowing through the pines outside the borrowed mansion. Beyond the walls and the room where the two musclemen waited behind me. I waited for Walter Maxwell Hardin's reaction to my question. He only swirled the brandy and soda slowly in his glass, began to talk almost to himself.

"I met her two years ago up at UCSB. The usual invitation to address the student body on business success and conservation theory, and the usual boring reception later where all the professors try to expound their particular hobby-horse ideas. Norma was there, one of the student hostesses assigned to shepherd me." He smiled as he remembered, drank his brandy. "I've been married three times, had more women friends than I can remember or ever forget, but I never met anyone else quite like Norma. A child and an earth mother. Innocent and older than time. Daughter, whore, and partner. Unique." He went on drinking the brandy and soda, but the smile was gone. "I'm not a boy and I'm not a fool. I know my age, and I admired her but left her there in the Faculty Club that night. We had talked half the night, I could see she knew what had happened, and I won't say I never thought of her over the next year, but I did nothing about it. I don't plunge into a questionable alliance ruled by emotion. In my position I can't and won't do that. So I forgot her, or I thought I had."

"Then?" I said.

He finished his brandy again. The Japanese did his act. Hardin didn't seem like a man who ordinarily drank as hard as he was drinking now. Many things make a man drink. One is to forget, another is to remember, and a third is to help him do something he doesn't want to do but knows he has to.

He examined his fresh drink. "I met her again by pure chance about a year ago. She was in trouble, came to see a lawyer who was one of mine. I happened to be there in his office that day. A chance in a million." He shook his head over the miracle of chance. "It was incredible, but there she was, and the moment I saw her again, I realized I had never forgotten her at all. Not for an instant over the whole year."

He thought that over behind the big desk, continued to drink. He would not be a man who had ever believed much in chance either. Or any fate except what he made happen for himself and others. To him it would have all seemed like a miracle. He would have had to believe that. A stroke of chance he would not let pass. Not lose. No matter what he had to do.

"I was in love." Shook his head in wonder. "That is quite a shock to a man in my position, a man of my age and habits. But I was in love, I knew it, and that was all there was to it." Now he looked across the desk at me, eye to eye. "I was in love with her, I wanted her, and when I make up my mind, Mr. Shaw, I act. The hell with the differences in our ages! Forget my past experiences with women, good and bad. I wanted her, and I want her. I intend to have her."

He sat there with his brandy, drank, and looked me straight in the eye. Firm and honest, even honorable. He was asking me, telling me, to understand him, understand his position. Understand what he had to do. Man to man. The way it had to be. For cause and country. In his case, for what he had to have, which for him was the same as cause and country.

"And she's no good to you in prison," I said. I didn't have much to lose by telling him what I knew, what I thought. "You're not a man who waits for what he wants, are you? Not if he can fix it so he doesn't have to wait. Norma could get a good jolt for that little pills scam, and even if she got off light, maybe one to five, that's a lot too long, right? So you started a campaign of lies and half truths and innuendo and delays and anything else you could think of to get her off scot-free, or at worst a few year's probation. You had those articles written and then paid Murray Engberg to publish them in *Western Ways*. It probably cost you a fair bundle. Editorial integrity doesn't come cheap in this country, even for a Murray Engberg. Just any old rag wouldn't do—it had to be a reputable journal, with national circulation. But the cost didn't matter to you. With enough brainwashing and propaganda in the media you can make the public believe anything. Maybe even put enough doubt into the minds of a district attorney or a judge. If you hammer hard enough and long enough on the same point, everyone will believe it's true and then it is true! Adolf Hitler's great discovery. Truth doesn't matter; only what you can make the masses believe is the truth. All you had to do was delay, influence, hammer away on Norma the poor victim, Norma the dupe, Norma the innocent pawn. With some judicious money and arm-twisting, of course."

The brandy didn't seem to be affecting him, but it had to be. Someplace where it didn't show. Like in his conscience, in his judgment of risk. But he wasn't ready to write me off as a hopeless case yet, as an egg he had to break. He still wanted to reason with an enemy who could become an ally.

"She was only a child when it began, Shaw. In some ways she's an ageless woman, but in others, in practical judgment, she's naive, an innocent. They led her into that wild spree, into crime and degradation. They duped her and led her straight to a jail cell and a courtroom. Asher first, then the others. At school she was in love with Asher, let him lead her on. She was all but kidnapped by Asher and Drake, fed drugs by Drake until she didn't know what she was doing. Until she didn't know right from wrong, was not responsible for what she did." It was essentially the whole story that had been in the *Western Ways* articles. Not the details, real or invented, but the thrust, the intent, the overall message. "I intend to get her off if it costs me a million, two million.

I knew the truth, but there was no way I could prove it. Those boys would only lie, were already lying. Norma told me the whole story that day in the lawyer's office, later at my house. I knew the truth, but no one else did. I had to create the proof, reveal the truth if I had to write it myself."

"Create proof with lies," I said. "The facts, what the boys said, what witnesses said, didn't matter. You knew the real truth and you would make everyone see it as you did no matter how many articles you had to fake, lies you had to tell, people you had to bribe. When that wasn't enough, you turned to murder. Jay Norca was triple trouble. A danger to Norma Powell, and if Norca killed Drake and Brownlee, you had no villain. It's not enough to just clear Norma; you have to offer the public a villain. And Norca was a part of the drug scheme, knew a lot too much, would look very bad in court."

Hardin put his glass down on the desk. There was something final about the action, the gesture. As if he had closed a door in his mind, sealed a contract. His eyes seemed to go blank, his face turn impassive. It was a face I expected his opponents had seen over the years.

"I'm going to save her, Shaw. She'll go free. I'll marry her."

"You can marry her," I said, "but I'm not sure you can save her. Not even you."

"I can try." He nodded to the two giants at the door.

"More murder?" I said.

"You don't give me much choice." He stood up. "I tried, Shaw."

And he was gone.

The two musclemen took my arms.

THIRTY-SIX

FACING AN UNSEEN enemy with death all around you isn't
something I want ever to do again after Nam, but I'd face
it a thousand times rather than stand helpless in the hands
of those who will kill me. Auschwitz. Kolyma. The Tower.
The Bastille. Death Row. Hopeless and helpless. Death in
an hour, tomorrow.

They marched me out of the gray stone mansion and into
the dark pines and redwoods. The faint light of dawn outlined the mountains across the valley below the mansion.
Unarmed, I walked in the hands of men with guns who had
killed at least one man I knew of. Walked where? A wall?
The shadows under a tree where a grave was already dug?

When? Ten minutes? An hour? A day? Now? This instant? Helpless . . .

Deep among the trees they sat me on the ground, stood
smoking and talking too low for me to hear. Looked at their
watches, looked at the sky lightening rapidly above the
mountains beyond the trees. The air was cool and clear,
clean to breathe. No smoke, no hot winds. A beautiful dawn
to be alive. Any dawn was good to be alive. Anywhere.

I stood up.

"Where the fuck are you going?"

I didn't know which one it was. Both looked at me, guns
in hand.

"You in a hurry?"

"Sit down, Shaw."

I sat. The light grew rapidly among the trees and I saw we
were close to the edge of the woods. Just beyond the trees
there was a long open field almost flat along the side of the
mountain. A field and a narrow blacktop road and wind-

sock on a pole and a small single-engine Beechcraft. The blacktop road was a runway. The two giants looked at the sky, motioned me up. We walked out of the trees toward the small plane.

They were going to take me away! A courtesy to the owner of the mansion? Honor among robber barons? No dirty work on loaned property? I didn't care what the reason was. It gave me time, and with time there is always a chance. Never wonder why a prisoner in an extermination camp, a slave camp, goes on doing what he is forced to do no matter how close he knows death to be. With time, there is always a chance.

One of them climbed into the Beechcraft. The other covered me from the ground.

"In."

I climbed in. The one in the plane handcuffed me to the rear seat. The one on the ground climbed into the pilot's seat. I watched him check the dials and gauges and levers as if not sure what they were all for. He got it started, we picked up wobbly speed, and the Beechcraft launched into uncertain flight.

For a long instant I sensed the climb was too sharp, the way it had so often been back in Nam with Charlie burning our tails. Then we leveled off shakily, and headed, as far as I could tell, northwest over the mountains.

"How long have you been flying this thing?" I asked.

Neither the pilot nor the one sitting next to me answered. They were both staring straight ahead.

"You sure you can keep it up and get it back down?"

The pilot said, "What do you care?"

The one beside me laughed. "That's good, Harry. That's pretty damn good. You're a comedian, Harry."

"It just came to me," the pilot, Harry said. "What's he care I can fly? I mean, what's he got to lose, right, Gabe?"

"Right," Gabe said. "He sure got nothin' to lose."

"It just come to me like that," Harry said.

"You're a comic, Harry," Gabe said.

The small plane wobbled, slewed on the drafts. Harry was a better comedian than he was a pilot. Hardin had probably told one of them to take flying lessons and Harry had lost. We seemed to veer more west, and the ground below changed into foothills and desert with a few scattered settlements.

"How much does Hardin pay for murder?" I said. "I hope it's plenty. You'll need all you can get at the trial."

Gabe grunted beside me. Harry seemed to fly steadier, as if thinking about something else helped.

"Someone's using Hardin, you know that," I said. "Someone's using him, and using you two, to get out of maybe worse than a drug-peddling fall."

Ahead smoke spread thick across the sky directly in our path.

"A lot of people know I'm investigating Hardin."

The small plane flew above the smoke of what had to be the fire in the San Gabriels behind the Valley and Los Angeles.

"I'm not working alone. I wasn't alone when you two grabbed me in Hermosa Beach. She saw you take me."

We were over the Valley, urban sprawl spread as far as the eye could see. An urban sprawl surrounded by fires. Behind us in the San Gabriels. To the left charring the Santa Monica Mountains. In Malibu and the canyons on the edge of the Pacific. Ahead inland from the Conejo Grade and somewhere beyond. A land on fire.

"You blew it on Jay Norca. Even the Hermosa Beach Police didn't believe it was an accident."

"We was in a hurry," Gabe said beside me. "We ain't in no hurry with you."

The pilot, Harry said, "No hurry no way. All the time in the world."

The fire below was to the right of the Conejo Grade, borate bombers and helicopters lumbering and swooping, firetrucks and hoses flung haphazardly along dirt back roads.

"When the time comes, you'll take the fall, not Hardin. I wasn't alone in that coffee house. She got your license."

Ahead, a fire burned in the back canyons around Santa Barbara and Montecito. The Beechcraft began to descend. It went down in a series of lurches, but it went down. Across a broad polo field with condominiums, golf courses. I recognized Montecito Village and knew where we were going. The landing strip was behind the big Italianate villa, behind the empty stables and the abandoned private polo ground.

Nose too high, the Beechcraft hit hard on the narrow runway, bounced, hit, bounced again, squealed tires, slewed, and, looking more like a kangaroo than an aircraft, slowly came to a stop. Harry stepped out onto the blacktop, gun drawn. Gabe unlocked my cuffs. The smell of smoke hung in the thick, ovenlike air.

"Out."

On the runway, Gabe prodded me ahead toward a small stone building among live oaks. He unlocked a heavy wooden door, swung it open, pushed me inside. The door locked behind me. I stood and listened. Outside the plane revved up and taxied away. I turned in a slow circle surveying the stone room. It was some kind of storeroom, with two tiny barred windows high up. Airless and stifling. Everything stone and thick except the massive wooden door and the floor. A wooden floor.

A wooden floor that gave under my weight. Springy. Not resting on either the ground or a concrete slab.

It took me ten minutes to find a board loose enough to pull up. The floor rested on nothing, on four-by-fours set into the dirt, the stone walls of the storeroom set down into the earth all around. It took me twenty more minutes, bathed in sweat, to rip up four boards, dig a few inches of dirt out and pile it on the floor next to the hole.

The Beechcraft returned slowly. I listened. It stopped outside the storeroom. Someone jumped out, came toward the storeroom. I picked up a board, stood behind the door.

Held the board in both hands, edge down to hit harder. The sweat poured off me now.

The door opened, "Okay, Shaw, time..."

Gabe saw the torn-up boards, the dirt on the floor. Ran to the hole. Reflex. Saw instantly that there was no hole, sensed the trick, half-turned. I hit him as hard as I could with the board, edge or flat I didn't have time to know. He went down, I went out. I turned for the trees.

"Far enough!" Harry stood just outside the door, gun in hand. "Walk on back."

Gabe came out of the storehouse. There was blood on his shirt collar, on his neat tie, but his eyes were clear. I'd hit him with the flat of the board. He had his gun aimed at my face.

"Not here," Harry said.

Gabe said, "He says do it! He says fuck who saw us, do it! Fuck who knows, we're covered!"

"Not here," Harry said.

Gabe breathed hard. "In the fucking plane!"

They handcuffed me again. Gabe sat beside me with his gun almost in my eye. Harry took the pilot seat. The Beechcraft taxied on to the end of the strip, revved up, wobbled and lurched into its takeoff like a wandering albatross. The only difference was that in the air the albatross is a magnificent soaring sight; we weren't. Harry barely cleared the trees at the end of the strip, but clear them he did, and...

The engine coughed, sputtered.

"Harry?" Gabe said.

The engine stopped. Started again. Sputtered.

"Harry!"

The engine stopped. The Beechcraft started down toward the dusty trees.

THIRTY-SEVEN

"JESUS, HARRY, GET—" Gabe said.

"Shut up!" Harry said. "Shut up."

"Harry!" Gabe cried.

Harry's teeth ground in the silence of rushing wind.

"We gotta turn back!" Gabe cried.

I said, "No. Fly straight ahead."

"Shut up! Shut up!"

"Turn it back!"

I kept my voice calm. "You can't turn. That's fatal. Fly straight, pick out somewhere to land."

Harry's eyes looked back. Terror and doubt.

"Land where, for shit's sake!"

"Turn the fucking thing!"

We all have our areas of helplessness. Defenseless and lost. Up in the air they had no control. Fear and panic. I spoke quietly, logically, reassuring.

"You don't have power to turn. You'll stall and crash. Straight ahead is the only chance. Glide until you can see an opening."

"How?"

"Glide shit!"

"What opening?"

I said, "Unlock me. I can fly enough to land it."

The Beechcraft sank lower.

"Do it," Harry said.

Gabe unlocked the handcuffs. I moved into the copilot's seat. Slowly, keeping balance. There were only trees. Almost close enough to touch. Endless trees. Ragged. Deadly.

A road.

Trees.

A church.

A fence.

A playing field!

I took the goddamn Beechcraft down. Gabe prayed.

"Shit! Shit! Shit!"

We went down. Hit hard. Bounced over a pitcher's mound. Sideswiped a batting cage. Lost a wing. Slewed drunkenly like a one-legged alcoholic. Slammed into a chain-link fence, almost flipped over, settled back shuddering in dust. I kicked the door open, rolled out to the ground. Gabe was already out the other side. Harry slumped over the controls.

"Harry!" Gabe leaned back in.

I ran.

"Harry! Come on, you motherfucker!"

I ran faster.

"Harry!"

At the edge of the playing field I looked back. Gabe was staggering away from the smoking Beechcraft with Harry in his arms. Flames exploded from the plane. Gabe went down on top of Harry. Sirens sounded somewhere close by. Gabe looked toward me, then looked away. Gabe had no interest in me now. Soon, but not now.

The fire engine from Montecito Village passed me. In the village I used the library pay phone. I didn't want to go back into the lion's mouth, but I had to. Walter Maxwell Hardin had the answers I needed, and I'd never get a safer time to ask the questions than now, with Harry and Gabe temporarily out of action.

Her voice came on the phone, "J.C. Connors."

"Paul Shaw. Can you pick me up in Santa Barbara? I found Doreen's Jack, and two killers are after me."

"Where are you?"

I told her. I waited inside the doors of the library after making sure there was a back way out. It took her twenty-six minutes, hang-up to walk-in. No one else appeared.

"Where do you want to go?"

"I'll show you in the car."

It was a battered gray Jaguar XJ12C.

"Loan from an old admirer."

We got in. I directed her away from where the Beechcraft was still smoldering, and through the twists and turns of the Montecito back road.

"Tell me," she said.

I told her what I had learned up at Folsom, but not about Hardin and Norma Powell. Not yet.

"Doreen's Jack was a crook? She brought those pills and those four kids together?"

"Jack Pointer," I said. "He was the missing link, the key to the whole thing."

"He killed Doreen? This Jack Pointer? Or his partner? What was the partner's name, Jay Norca?"

"I don't think so," I said. "And Pointer sure didn't kill Norca."

"Then who?" she said. "I never believed she killed herself—now I know. Caught in some kind of fast shuffle. Who, Shaw?"

"I'm working on it. Stop here."

We were in front of the high iron gates of Monte Oro, with its smaller peasant houses all around. High, locked gates, an equally high wall in both directions. The smell of fire.

"Drive along that way."

Toward the mountains, where there seemed to be fewer houses around the wall. Gabe and Harry had left me in the stone shed to consult someone about what I had told them. That I had not been alone, would be missed. That people knew I was investigating Hardin, that my confederate had their license. Someone at Monte Oro. Even if Hardin wasn't here, maybe I could talk to him over the closed circuit. And it should be the last place Gabe and Harry would look for me when their minds were back on the job.

"There!"

J.C. Connors parked in front of the small break in the wall. Just a gap in the top of the wall where a tree had fallen in some winter storm. Hardin wasn't Mafia or CIA or Soviet embassy, so his security didn't have to be that tight. Not until now. The odor of fire was stronger here. Sirens wailed in the distance.

"Go back and watch the front gate," I said. "If you see anyone go in, let them get out of sight and then honk like mad."

"Who the hell owns this place?"

"A man called Walter Maxwell Hardin. A very rich man."

"Yeah," she said, stared across the wall. "Where does he fit into all this?"

"He's in love with Norma Powell, working to get her off. That's all I know so far."

"Norma?" She went on staring at the wall. "How old is he?"

"That's the problem," I said. "Don't forget to hit the horn if anyone goes through those gates. Anyone."

I crossed the road and slipped over the wall through the narrow gap in the top half. Inside, I trotted through the forest of oak and eucalyptus as silently as I could, hoped Hardin didn't use guard dogs I hadn't seen. At the edge of the trees I looked at the rear of the gigantic Tuscan palace across the abandoned polo field and stables. Groundskeepers worked at the distant edge of the lawn. I could hear machines somewhere in the trees a long way off. The fire was still over the first ridge of mountains beyond the estate, but Hardin would be preparing his defenses just in case. There was no one between me and the house.

I left the trees, walked across the polo field. A running man attracts attention.

The garages were all closed.

The same side door was open.

Along the dark corridor of the old servants' quarters, I moved toward the rectangle of light that was the kitchen.

There was no one in the vast kitchen. No one in the marble halls and rotunda with its fountains and niches. The door to the small closed-circuit television room was open. I went in, closed the door behind me.

"Are you looking for me, Mr. Shaw?"

THIRTY-EIGHT

NORMA POWELL SAT at the desk in front of the closed-circuit TV. She didn't seem surprised to see me. Smoked, looked at the dark television set and out over the lawn.

"If you want Maxie, he's not here. Just me and the butler."

"You'll do," I said. "You're not surprised I'm here?"

Once more, a different Norma Powell. In white silk lounging pajamas, her hair up in a French twist. Bracelets and rings and silver high-heeled slippers. Cool eyes that looked at me without any of her earlier shyness or diffidence. No confusion at all. The innocent waitress and the Ivy Leaguer both gone. Now she looked older than her years.

"Only a little." She looked out at the lawn again. "I thought you'd be figuring it out about now."

I sat in a white wicker chair. She didn't know I'd talked to Hardin—he hadn't told her—and Gabe and Harry hadn't talked to her either. If Hardin wasn't in the house, they had contacted him on the closed-circuit TV without telling Norma Powell what they were doing. I lit a cigarette.

"It wasn't that hard to figure," I said. "Someone was trying to make you look like Little Red Riding Hood in those *Western Ways* articles. There had to be something phony about them: an invisible author, no one in them talking, Drake and Brownlee laughing at them, Murray so scared of questions he tried to kill me. The only reason that made sense was to try to create public opinion, influence judge, jury, and even prosecutor; and the only one helped was you. The poor little duped girl. Faking a series of articles in a major magazine would take money and power. That fitted Hardin, and he was already in the case trying to influence me. He didn't supply those pills, and it didn't look like he had any reason to help any of your parents."

She continued to smoke. One arm hugged her own waist as if she were cold in the air-conditioned mansion.

"He wants to marry me. May and September."

"More like January and December."

"Love conquers all."

"Money and power helps," I said.

"It always has."

I said, "So he wants you, and he doesn't want to wait ten years. At his age, not even two to five with time off for good behavior. He used his money to get Murray Engberg to publish slanted articles and try to brainwash everyone in your favor. He used his power to get the trial delayed to give his faked propaganda time to work. A good lawyer or ten, pressure in the right places, maybe even a bribe or two. Anything and everything so he doesn't have to wait five years for his tootsie."

She put out her cigarette. She smiled at me. "Not getting any younger, is he? But he won't have to wait. He paid Engberg to publish those articles. He got the delays. Not that the story in those articles isn't true all the way. It's just that Maxie doesn't leave anything to chance. He says the truth alone doesn't always win. He says you have to help the truth out. You have to make sure people know what's true, maybe fix things up a little so they know the real truth. But those articles are essentially true. The boys were the leaders. I went along like a fool girl." She lit another cigarette. "He'll get me off all the way. Little Norma, squeaky clean. Free as a bird with old Walter Maxwell Hardin. And not a damn thing you or anyone can do about it. He's got too much muscle, so go home. You can't beat him."

"I wasn't hired to beat him. I was hired to find who killed Robert Asher."

"That gunman in my cottage killed Robbie."

"Hardin tell you that?"

"He did. No more worry for me, no more case for you, right? He's dead, you can go back to New York."

"His partner isn't dead. The other one you stole the pills from."

She smiled at me. "He will be if he comes around here."

"Just like that?"

"You believe it. When Maxie wants something, he gets it." She looked out at the lawn and drive again. As if she expected to see someone, wanted to see someone before he saw her.

"You expect Hardin back soon?"

"Max is out of the country."

I didn't tell her I knew better. She was alert to see someone, and my guess was that it was Walter Hardin. Because she wasn't supposed to talk to me? Or was it someone else? A different worry. Perhaps a visitor she didn't want me to meet.

"You haven't told your parents about Hardin?"

"I told them."

"Your father didn't seem to know."

"My father does what I tell him to do." She laughed, blew smoke as she watched the window and the lawn. "He's a nice man, my father, a gentleman. He's never done anything in his whole life. Nothing. Neither he nor my mother. Done nothing and are nothing."

She got up, walked to the window, but whatever she was watching for wasn't there.

"Hardin set you up in the cottage, the club?"

She laughed again. "As poor and innocent as possible. If anyone knew about us, it would hurt me. Juries don't like rich men or their girlfriends. He wanted to be sure I got a fair trial."

"Maybe a little more than fair."

"Now it doesn't matter—the trial is next week."

I wasn't sure Hardin would agree with her. But then, I wasn't sure it was her real reason for dropping her cover.

"I told Hardin about Doreen Connors."

She returned to her chair at the TV set. "So?"

"He didn't know about her."

"Why should he? I expect a whole lot of people don't know about Doreen."

"Eliot Drake knows about her."

"He was there," she said.

"Brownlee says Drake has a big scheme to make their fortune, make them rich. With his 'little partner,' Drake's going to make them both rich."

She lit another cigarette. "That proves it, doesn't it? Drake and his goddamn get-rich-quick schemes. Every time. First the four of us; now it's just Brownlee he'll lead up the path. You see?"

"What happened to Asher as the evil genius?"

She was up again and at the door. If she heard me, she didn't have an answer, or didn't care. The door opened and the old butler came in. She must have used a hidden button.

"I have to go out," she said. "Mr Hardin just told me he wanted Shaw kept here."

"Very good, madam."

She'd do fine as the wife of Walter Maxwell Hardin, despite the age difference. A born aristocrat. She went out into the marble of the Roman palace Hardin called a house. I went after her. Or I started to.

"Please sit down, Mr. Shaw," the old butler said.

He had a gun.

THIRTY-NINE

"SHE'S LYING TO YOU," I said. "She never talked to Hardin."

He cocked the pistol.

"Sit down, Mr. Shaw."

I sat down.

"Would you care for some coffee?"

"Why not?"

He crossed to the desk in front of the TV screen, reached under. That was where the button was.

"She never turned on the set," I said.

He sighed and sat facing me. Uncocked the pistol but held it steady and looked like he knew how to use it.

"You take your orders from her now?"

"So I have been instructed."

"Orders about business?"

I saw the flicker in his eyes. There was a diffident knock at the door.

"Come in," the butler said.

A young Mexican boy came in carrying the same silver coffee service on its silver tray. They had a signal that meant bring coffee. Efficient and time-saving. Walter Maxwell Hardin didn't wait for anything. The boy stared at the gun in the butler's hand. The butler made a sharp grunt and the boy hurriedly poured a cup of coffee. The butler grunted again. The boy put in cream and one teaspoon of sugar, carried the cup and saucer to me. I smiled. The boy didn't. A third grunt sent him out of the room. One cup of coffee. The old butler did not join the guests.

"Nice coffee," I said.

"Thank you," the butler said.

"You always carry a gun around the house?"

"Mr. Hardin suggests it for when he is away."

"British army?"

"That was a long time ago, Mr. Shaw."

"She *was* lying, you know," I said. "She's gone somewhere she doesn't want me to know. I'm not sure she wants Hardin to know."

"Gabe and Harry will return soon. They can decide what Mr. Hardin would want." He almost smiled. "On a business matter."

"You know where they went?"

"No, Mr. Shaw. Off in the Beechcraft somewhere. As you surmised, Mr. Hardin does usually keep me separate from his business ventures."

I drank the coffee. It was still good, but I enjoyed it less now. I was lucky Hardin kept him out of business—he didn't know I'd been with Gabe and Harry in the Beechcraft. But I didn't want to wait for Gabe and Harry.

"That could be too late," I said. "If my hunch is right about where she's gone, Miss Powell could be in real danger."

"Danger?"

I nodded. "I don't know how much you know, but she was involved in a drug deal, and I think she's gone to meet with one of her partners in that deal who isn't exactly stable."

"I see." I got the flicker in the eyes again, and this time a faint doubt in his voice, a hesitation.

"How important is she to Hardin?"

"Quite important, yes."

"Then—"

"Then what, Mr. Shaw?"

"Well, maybe you should ask him."

He had spent a lifetime being impassive, neutral, part of the furniture, the walls.

"Ask him what?"

"If he wants me kept here when she could be in danger and I know where she's gone. At least I could tell him what I know, and he could get in touch with Gabe and Harry and send them."

"You can tell him where she is now?"

"I can make a good guess." Never overdo it.

"Perhaps I can reach him."

"I hope so," I said, concerned.

He nodded. Stood up without taking his eyes off me or lowering the pistol. He would have been a good soldier, and some things you never forget. He turned on the closed-circuit TV, waited for it to warm up, pushed various buttons under the desk in front of it. The screen flipped through different empty rooms until Walter Maxwell Hardin's face finally appeared in a room I didn't recognize. He looked out of the set, puzzled and irritated.

"Yes, what is it, Lovat?"

"I have Mr. Shaw here, sir." He looked back at me.

I moved into camera range beside the butler. "Here, Mr. Hardin."

"Shaw? How did he . . . ? What's going on, Lovat?"

The butler, Lovat, looked at the camera. "He came to see Miss—"

I had the gun, kicked the butler in the stomach. Knocked the pistol away, hit him on the nose. Down, he was bleeding.

"Stop him!" Hardin raged from the screen. He stared at his set in the distant room. "Lovat! Stop him!"

I had the pistol, waved to the camera.

"Shaw, you—"

Hardin raged, sputtered on the screen.

I turned off the set, bent down over the butler. The blood was only from his nose. He held his stomach where I'd kicked.

"You okay?"

He sat up slowly. "Too old," he said.

"Anything broken?"

He shook his head, breathed. I found a box of tissues, worked on his nose.

"Much too old."

"Everybody's too old or too young for something."

"You tricked me neatly. Time to retire."

His nose would look like a banana in the morning, but it wasn't broken and I had the bleeding stopped.

"I'm going to tie you up."

"Of course."

There were enough electric cords in the room to tie an army. I left him tied to the heavy desk, and got out of there as fast as I could. Gabe and Harry would return sometime.

The marble corridors, the enormous kitchen, and the dim back hall were deserted. Nothing was outside the side door except a thick wall of heat and drifting smoke, but one of the garage doors was open now, the space inside empty. I walked back across the overgrown polo field, past the silent stables into the trees. The smell of smoke from the fire up in the mountains was suddenly stronger. The wind had changed, blew now out of the canyons. Hardin's men were going to have their hands full soon.

On the other side of the wall I trotted along the road toward the front gates of Hardin's estate. Cars and trucks passed me going toward the mountains. Everyone in them held shovels and axes, looked up at the sky to see the wind. All of Montecito was going to have its hands full unless the down-canyon winds changed again.

I reached the front gates. They were closed and locked. J.C. Connors wasn't there. I looked all along the road on both sides, up two cross roads. The old Jaguar wasn't anywhere. I started walking toward Santa Barbara. An empty flatbed truck picked me up. A fire makes people helpful. He dropped me in front of a Hertz office downtown. Half an hour later I was on the freeway headed south.

By the time I reached the Conejo Grade, the traffic crawled up the long, steep curves. Thick smoke blew across the twists and turns, and halfway up I saw the flames not a quarter of a mile to the left down in the deep canyons between the high ridges. I smelled burning wood, and grass, and flesh through the windows. The flesh of animals dead in the fire. Innocent victims of real-estate greed and human stupidity.

Overhead the borate bombers swept in low to drop their red clouds of fire-retardant, the helicopters hovered with men and equipment and great smothering masses of water. All along the crest of the ridges to the east, the firefighters in their yellow hardhats dug and chopped and ran from hot spot to hot spot. The flames crept up either side of them like a Zulu army encircling the enemy to trap them in a sudden firestorm that would destroy them.

Then I was up over the crest of the grade and going downhill in the clear air of the Conejo Valley where the fires had not yet reached. Drove on toward a different firestorm about to destroy other people.

FORTY

ELIOT DRAKE'S JENSEN-HEALY was parked in the alley behind the three-story gray frame house on Pelican Lane. I went up. From the top you could see the fire in Santa Monica. The door was locked. I looked at the locked door for some time, listened. There was no sound from the apartment. I took out my ring of keys and went to work on the lock I'd never seen locked before.

I stopped.

The sound came from inside.

Like something being dragged slowly across the floor. Something heavy. Some large animal moving around the room inside, breathing carefully. An aimless movement, in no particular direction. Only moving. Breathing.

I braced against the railing of the open landing and kicked the door open. Jumped in and right. The room was empty. Except for the slow, aimless movement of something heavy somewhere.

I found him behind the long couch that faced the windows toward the sea. Crawling. Just crawling. A foot or two one way, a foot or two the other way. Hal Brownlee, his head moving back and forth like a blind worm searching for the source of some heat, some sound. Blood covered the bare wood floor around him, led back in a bloody trail to the table in the small kitchen area. I bent over him. He didn't seem to know I was there, kept on crawling aimlessly, searching for nothing, going nowhere.

He had been shot twice. Once in the left side, once in the upper arm. The side wound was in as good a place as any bullet wound could be, had almost stopped bleeding even with his crawling. I put a tourniquet on his arm above the

wound, looked him over for any other injuries that might
make it dangerous to move him any more than he was moving himself. I found nothing, sat him up with his back
against the couch.

In the kitchen I located a bottle of ammonia in the cabinet under the sink. I opened it and moved it under Brownlee's nose. He was breathing so lightly, moving his head, it
took three tries for the fumes to hit him.

"Wha...!" He coughed violently, gagged, choked,
coughed again. His eyes opened. Panicked eyes. "What...?
Eliot?"

"Brownlee? Who shot you?"

He shook his head violently, groaned in pain, gagged and
coughed. "Eliot...don't..."

"Was it Drake? Did Drake shoot you?"

He coughed and the pain hit his eyes and he passed out
against the couch.

I searched the rooms and the bedrooms. Eliot Drake was
in the second bedroom. He crouched small in the far corner like a frightened dog trying to hide. His head tucked
down and behind his arm as if he hoped to be invisible. He
looked a lot smaller, but not small enough. Not invisible.
There was less blood but more damage. He was dead. Shot
twice also. The killer's aim had been better this time: one
bullet in the head, one in the chest.

Brownlee was still unconscious on the floor with his back
against the shabby couch. I loosened the tourniquet, used
the ammonia again. His eyes opened, he coughed, then
grunted at the pain of the cough. He looked up at me, but
he didn't recognize me. He didn't care. He didn't care who
I was. I was there. There and helping him, and he would
have talked to anyone who was there and helping him. To
talk. To know he was alive.

"Brownlee?" I said, crouched down close to his pale face.
"What happened?"

He sat staring at me until the pain eased out of his eyes. I
retightened the tourniquet. He breathed in soft, light, shal-

low breaths. If he breathed harder, he would crumble in the silent apartment.

"...had a...gun. She...tried to stop...her. Shot...shot Eliot...looked...looked..."

"Looked at what?"

His eyes blinked up at me. Vague.

"Looked at what? For what?"

The drained face of a confused child. "She...looked...all...over...I...not...move...gone...Eliot...crawled...Eliot?" I spoke gently, quietly. Crouched down where he was sitting, touched him, and spoke softly to his face.

"Start from the beginning. She came to the apartment. She had a gun. Who was she? Who had a gun?"

He looked at me as if trying very hard to understand what I was saying. The eyes of an obedient dog watching its master speak to it. "Eliot said...it was...time. The trial...too late...talk to her...tell her...we...get...rich...come...alone...rich..."

He stopped, more from lack of breath than anything else. I loosened the tourniquet again. He closed his eyes against the pain, breathed harder.

"Who, Brownlee? Who was she? How are you going to get rich?"

The pain curtained his eyes, shock and fear. His eyes opened straight at me and there was no recognition. "Stuff...her stuff...had it...Eliot..."

"Brownlee? It's Paul Shaw. Who shot you? Who was she?"

I tightened the tourniquet once more. His side had started to bleed again. His eyes glanced around the room as if looking for someone. I was losing him. The effort had been too much.

"Brownlee? Tell me her name. Name, Brownlee."

It was no use. His eyes had closed and his head lolled against the couch. He was unconscious again and I didn't have that much time. I found the telephone, called the police and paramedics. Then I sat beside him. I stanched the side wound, loosened and tightened the tourniquet. I wanted to leave, chase the killer. There wasn't a lot of time if the killer was one of the three possibles. But helping the innocent is more important that catching the guilty.

Until I heard sirens through the hot afternoon air. Different sirens blending and clashing. I waited until they slowed to turn into the street below. Then I hurried out and down the stairs to the alley and my rented car. I would apologize to Jacoby later. I could be too late already.

FORTY-ONE

THE FREEWAYS TOOK me once more to North Hollywood
and the twisting road up to Sandra Peterson's apartment on
the lip of its hill. In the distance the smoke of the Santa
Monica Mountain fire seemed to be thinning for the first
time, but farther to the north the smoke still darkened the
late-afternoon sky.

There was no answer at her door. Her car wasn't there.
Mine was. It was parked in the driveway beside the house.
She had found my keys, maybe even got the license number
of Hardin's limousine. That was something I could use.

I retrieved my Colt Agent from under the front seat,
looked at my watch. It was a few minutes after four o'clock.
I lit a cigarette and smoked and watched my smoke and the
fire smoke drift across the yellowish sky on the hot wind.

Four-fifteen. If she was working, she wouldn't be home
until sometime around five-thirty. If she was working.

In the distance where the fire had swept down the slopes
of the Santa Monica Mountains, taking the trees and bushes
with it, the sounds seemed to be louder, to come more
clearly across the city. Trees and bushes are natural sound
deadeners, and from the stripped slopes, even across the
city, I could hear the small sounds of clanking vehicles,
shovels and picks that worked in invisible canyons to stop
the flames in their tracks.

At four-thirty Sandra had not come home.

On the other side of the house perched precariously on the
edge of its hill, across the canyons below and the whole San
Fernando Valley, the far-off fire in the high San Gabriels
burned all along the skyline. Smoke towered into the sky.
We are an arrogant species. We insist that our need is the

measure of everything. If we need, and can do what is necessary, then we must have.

Five o'clock. If she were working, she should be no later than five-thirty, perhaps six.

It is our right to build houses too high on dry hillsides, even if we bring fire and burn out not only ourselves but every other living thing there also. It is our right to live by selling this dry land for purposes it should not be used for. It is our right to use the water to wash our cars, to destroy the delicate balance of nature to build our houses.

Five-fifteen. Somewhere a man and a woman talked, argued. Someone was singing.

What we need we will have, must have, even if we destroy the land and the water and the air until there is no longer any land worth having, any water that can be drunk safely, any air left to breathe except perhaps in small pockets where we can sit and gasp away our last few days as a species on a dead earth.

Our wants are our needs, and our needs become our destiny.

At five-thirty I heard the car coming slowly up the twists and turns.

I went out to the edge of the driveway. The car continued to climb toward me. It could turn off in at least two places. I listened as it passed the last side road. It did not turn. At the cul-de-sac just below the final rise to this house, the car slowed. I waited. It did not turn off, came steadily on and around the last curve to slow and turn into the driveway beside me. Sandra looked out.

"You're all right?"

"I'm all right. It was Hardin. We talked."

"I'll bet," she said. "I've been waiting for you to come back, hoping. I didn't know what to do. Police or what."

"Where've you been?" I asked. "Today. The last hour or so."

"Been? At work. Where else would I be?"

She had no punk wig on, and her dark hair was pulled back at the nape of her neck the way she always wore it to work in her office. A demure gray dress, hose, high heels. Her proper office clothes. It would be simple to check if she had been at work, if she had ever left for an hour or so. She would know that.

"I'm going to search your car," I said.

"All right," she said. She got out. "What's happened, Paul?"

"Drake's been killed, Brownlee shot. In Hermosa Beach. Maybe an hour from here."

I searched the car. I gave it a thorough search. There was no gun. She could have thrown it out, but she had no way of knowing I would be at the house.

"They were shot because Drake had another scheme to get rich. I think it was blackmail this time. He had something. Some evidence, I expect. Something he thought was worth a lot of money. Something his 'little partner' would help him turn into gold."

She watched me. "Where would I get the kind of money Drake would consider enough to call getting rich?"

I said, "I had to be sure."

"Are you?"

"Yes."

"Then we can talk. I want to talk, Paul. I'll make some dinner, open a wine."

"I'd like that," I said. "Later. Now I have to drive north again. I'll be back. Maybe tonight, maybe tomorrow, but I'll be back."

"I'll watch your car."

I nodded. "Can you give me the license number of that limousine they used to snatch me?"

She gave it to me. "Maybe you can work out here more."

"Every year there's more cases," I said.

"You could discuss it with your partners."

"I could," I said.

She still sat in her car when I drove away.

FORTY-TWO

THE DRIVE DOWN the Conejo Grade was a nightmare. A single lane in each direction, crawling in the oven heat and choking smoke. Both lanes were on the southbound side. Drivers swearing, passengers sweating and leaning out windows. Smoke and even flames as fingers of the fire licked up the steep canyon slopes almost to the edge of the freeway.

The closed northbound lanes looked like the front line of a war. The firefighters' vehicles lined up like tanks, highway patrol cars parked all the way down the grade. The khaki-uniformed patrolmen violently waved the traffic on, commanded it to halt as a wall of smoke swept across, urged it to hurry past again. Fire engines stood parked everywhere. Hoses piled and tangled in slippery masses. The old bombers swooped in low for air cover. Helicopters hovered. The firefighters shoveled, chopped, hosed.

If the fire jumped the highway, it would go on forever. The road would have to be closed. So the battle in the northbound lanes was a last-ditch stand, holding the ridge, and nothing but the endless pressure of the cars that could not be rerouted without a fantastic traffic jam back in the Valley made the police allow the single lane through in each direction.

When I finally reached the bottom and Camarillo, it was dark and the traffic, released, was light and clear all the way into Ventura where the fires had gone in the other direction into the mountains away from the sea. At the Holiday Inn J.C. Connors did not answer the house phone, and her old Jaguar wasn't in the parking garage.

The Club Chicago was packed. The owner, Barney, stood at the bar looking at the clock. He did not seem happy. I ordered a Beck's. Barney saw me.

"You know maybe where she is?"

"Norma Powell?"

"J.C., damn it. She's on in half an hour."

The beer washed the smoke from my parched throat. "When did you see her last?"

"Last night. She missed rehearsal. I mean, that's no fucking sweat—she's missed rehearsal before and it's her idea anyway. Me, I don't figure she needs rehearsal; save her pipes. Now it's half an hour to first show, I've got a club full of paying customers waiting to hear her, and where the fuck is she?"

"No one's seen her today?"

He looked again at the clock. It had moved one minute. He swore. "She won't work west of Hoboken, so help me."

"You don't have that kind of muscle."

He shrugged. "Don't I know it. She don't show, I'm fucked, and all I can do is yell and hope she shows tomorrow. It makes me feel better. Yelling and thinking about what the hell I'm going to do to her."

"No one saw her since last night?"

"One of the waiters. Saw the Jag heading north maybe two hours ago."

"North?"

"That's what he said. He don't speak English so good, but I guess he can tell direction." He waved to the bartender for a drink. It was a new bartender. Bartenders he could fire. "Two hours, I figured she got plenty of time. So where the fuck is she?"

"Where did the waiter see her?"

"Out front."

"Doing what? Passing by? Parked?"

"Like she'd been to her dressing room for something. Got into the Jag and headed off toward the freeway north." His drink came, he gulped it. "I'll lose eighty percent of 'em soon as we announce she ain't gonna sing. Maybe ninety percent tomorrow if word gets around she wasn't here tonight and maybe won't be tomorrow night. Damn!"

"Did he see her arrive? The waiter."

He shook his head. "I don't know. I don't think so."

"Where is he?"

"Who?" He finished his drink, pushed the glass to the bartender. He was getting up his courage for the announcement that J.C. Connors would not appear at the eight o'clock show, maybe not at all.

"That waiter."

He searched the room. "Over there. Table six. Eufemio."

I left him starting on his second drink and staring up at the bar clock. It was seven-forty-five. He drank, looked at the crowded club, drank again.

The waiter, Eufemio, was a skinny kid with a Mayan nose and the barest hint of a mustache trying to grow. I stopped him on his way to the kitchen, told him the boss had sent me. He nodded, polite and eager to help.

"You saw Miss Connors today?"

"*Si,* yes, in car. She go to north."

Eufemio smiled, nodded. The boy was proud of his English. That meant he was Mexican, an illegal probably.

"Did you see where she came from?"

The boy paled. Stared at me.

"When you saw her first, was she driving the car?"

"North," the boy said. "I see."

"Where was the car?"

"In front. She go in, go north."

The club owner must have told the boy the word *north*.

The boy had pointed, and the owner had said, "North?" The boy had smiled and said, "Si, north," and that was a new word he remembered well, but his English wasn't good enough for the rest I needed to know. I smiled.

"Thank you, Eufemio. *Gracias.*"

Eufemio beamed. "*De nada.*"

At the bar the owner, Barney, was staring at the clock on the wall as if he couldn't stop himself, frozen by the inexorable passage of time and the arrival of his moment of doom. Like a small animal watching the slow approach of some soft-footed predator about to pounce. The clock read 7:59.

I left the club. If my guess was right, there was only one place to the north she would go. Walter Maxwell Hardin's estate.

FORTY-THREE

IN SANTA BARBARA the fire was still in the mountains behind Montecito, the flames licking up the dark slopes and darker night. The wind only moved the scorching heat against my face. Sweat and the smell of burned wood, a distant sound of exploding eucalyptus, of fiery chaparral that crackled and snapped.

Firefighters and equipment filled the back roads like the crush and confusion of an advancing army bringing up new troops. The dark gates of Monte Oro stood open, outlined in an eerie light by the far-off flicker of flames on the slopes behind the great estate. Some of the firefighting vehicles passed through and on toward the big house. They would help hold the line behind Monte Oro. There was something isolated about the silent estate behind its walls, indifferent to the flames but vulnerable, too, besieged.

I pushed the button on the wall.

"Yes?" It was the butler's calm, imperturbable voice.

"Paul Shaw," I said. "I want to talk to Hardin."

"I see. Just a moment, Mr. Shaw."

If the fire swept down, swept Monte Oro into oblivion, the butler would walk quietly out with the silver and his gun to drive off any attacks on it if necessary. Because it was his job. Monte Oro and the Hardins might vanish, but not the silver. And the moment was a long moment. Very long.

"Drive directly to the house, Mr. Shaw. To the same side door. I'm sure you know it by now."

I took my little Colt from its holster, put it into my jacket pocket, and drove up through the forest of oak and palm and eucalyptus ghostly in the light from the far-off fire. The dark lawn seemed somehow desolate, as if it had lost its reason for being. Simply a vast expanse of grass without purpose.

The great house, too, as I drove around it. Enormous and shadowy in the night, but cold, without lights or life. Barren, as if it needed its hordes of vanished servants to come alive again. The piratical masters and their army of guests who had vacationed here from the rigors of making fortunes. The forgotten players in the polo matches. The captains of industry who came to play golf in privacy with the born rich they needed for status. The born rich here to play billiards and drink champagne on the night terraces with the money they needed. The sound of music and dancing and privileged voices through its echoing halls.

The butler, Lovat, and Gabe waited in front of the garages. Lovat had a blackened eye and a swollen nose where I'd hit him. Gabe had his gun. Three garage doors were open. The limousine was there. The green Honda and the Jaguar weren't. I slipped my little Colt out of my pocket and under the front bucket seat before I got out. Gabe walked to meet me.

"How's Harry?" I said.

"He'll live," Gabe said.

He frisked me expertly, in control here. Stepped back.

"You should have stayed away."

"Sometimes you can't do what you should."

He waved the gun. "Inside."

Lovat led the way once more along the dim servants' quarters corridor into the vast kitchen and out through the marble halls and the entrance rotunda to the cozy paneled office/study/closed-circuit TV room. Walter Maxwell Hardin stood with his back to the windows, outlined by the glow of flames on the dark mountains behind the great house. I could see far-off shadows capering against the glow of the fire. The firefighters. Hardin seemed to watch them.

"Where is she, Shaw?"

"I came to ask you."

Hardin shook his head. "No. Lovat says you knew where she was going this afternoon."

"I knew then," I said. "I don't know now."

"I suggest you think very hard. If you don't know where she is, you're no good to me and shouldn't have come back here."

Gabe laughed. "He got a death wish."

"Shut up!" Hardin looked at the big muscleman with the cold, hard eyes that had turned millions into billions. Sullen, Gabe leaned against the wall near the door. Angry at me. I'd made his boss abuse him, show him up.

"She should be here," I said. "Where else could she go for help?"

Hardin came away from the window. "She isn't."

He wore his banker's uniform: three-piece blue cashmere pin-stripe, white shirt, regimental tie, gold watch chain, polished black shoes, single heavy gold signet ring with at least a three-carat diamond. As if in full uniform for the final act, the last negotiation.

"If she were in trouble," I said, "where else could she go?"

Hardin watched me for almost a full minute. Outside, through the windows, I saw helicopters in the night, a sheriff's car, trucks and running men, all moving across the vast open space of the estate toward the fire. They would save the great house. Hardin didn't seem to care.

"What kind of trouble?" Hardin said.

"That depends on what she's done," I said. "If she's a killer or a victim."

Hardin sat down in a high-backed leather lounge chair. He did not look good. Somehow smaller. Gabe leaned back against his wall in that almost-asleep pose gunmen seem to favor. The *pistolero* of the Old West waiting for the showdown. Everyone's seen too many movies.

Hardin said, "What do you think she could have done?"

"Eliot Drake is dead down in Hermosa Beach. He was shot a few hours ago by a woman. She shot Hal Brownlee, too, but he isn't dead. He's alive, and he said enough before he passed out for me to know Drake had some evidence against the woman, was blackmailing her. Brownlee's not going to die, the police have him, and sooner or later he'll tell them who the woman was.''

Hardin said, ''What evidence?''

''My guess is that a year ago Doreen Connors was murdered to stop her from blowing the pills deal. I think Drake had evidence to prove it, so Doreen's murderer killed Drake, and Brownlee knows where the evidence is and who killed Drake. If it was Norma, the police'll be up here sooner or later. They could be right behind me.''

Gabe came alert at the wall. Hardin seemed to shrink even smaller as he fixed his stare on me.

''How much?'' Hardin said. ''You know I can give you whatever it takes. I can make you a rich man. Get back in your car, drive away, forget anything you know about Norma Powell. You never came here, you know nothing. Tell the police nothing. Without you, I can deal with the police.''

''They know I found Drake and Brownlee, or they will.''

''You can think of something to tell them.''

''It doesn't matter anyway, Hardin. Brownlee's alive.''

He looked twenty years older now than that night in the pub in Santa Monica. Just an old man with his needs. An old man fighting to keep what made him feel young.

''You're not sure it was Norma, and Brownlee's badly wounded, could still die. The woman who shot Drake could have been someone else.''

''An outside chance. Doreen Connors's mother is out here. She could have shot Drake and Brownlee, revenge for her daughter. But that still leaves the killing of Doreen Connors herself. Drake was blackmailing someone.''

There was a haunted hope in his sagging eyes. ''Drake's dead. No one has to know if Norma killed that Connors girl. My lawyers and some cash can handle Brownlee. As long as no one is *sure* she killed anyone, I can fix it. A reasonable doubt. You can be richer than your wife.''

Gabe shifted against the wall, made a sound. A protest grunt. A man didn't beg. Not for a woman.

I said, ''If she did it all or not, Hardin, she's using you. She probably hung around your lawyer's office a month to arrange her 'accidental' meeting. She wanted your money, your power, your influence, and she set out to get it. She's used you from the start and every step of the way. She hasn't even played it clean. Ask the manager of The Club Chicago.''

Gabe made another sound. Almost like approval. The butler, Lovat, appeared in the doorway.

''The sheriff's office is on the telephone, sir. They wish to speak to you. They asked if Miss Powell were here.''

Gabe made another sound. He was becoming almost loquacious. I had a hunch this sound meant that he had no liking for a battle with the police. Not in the open. Lovat was impassive, awaiting orders. Hardin seemed to regroup, grow stronger again. He had a concrete problem, something he could attack.

''She's not here. I'm too busy to see them. Tell them to keep their minds on the fire. Stall them.''

''Very good, sir.''

Hardin was up, walked around the small room. ''I know what she's doing, what she is. I'm old and alone. I want her and I need her and I don't care how I get her or what she needs from me. She told me everything that first day in the lawyer's office, what she wanted me to do. I told her what I needed. We've both kept our bargains as best we could. I don't know that she has killed anyone. I don't believe she has killed anyone.''

My English grandmother always said, *With the rich and mighty, a little patience.* Because they don't know that the rules apply to them. They're above the rules. How could they believe anything else? Then or now. Then they were lords; the world they knew belonged to them, literally. Now, with a president guilty of more than one crime; another who lied and tricked his own Congress into a war; a senator who thinks it's okay to steal another country fair and square; cabinet members, governors, mayors, and a million and one businessmen accused of every crime and shady deal in the book in their own self-interest, what else could they believe? If you have power, privilege, there are no rules. It starts with stop signs and ends with murder.

"Would it make any difference if you did know?" I said.

There was almost an excitement in his eyes. "I don't think it would. I've waited too long for a woman like her. As tough as I am. Young. Beautiful. I won't let you or anyone else—"

We all heard the motors. First one, then a second. Somewhere in the direction of the abandoned polo field behind the great house. Aircraft engines.

FORTY-FOUR

ONE OF THE planes fighting the fire? Forced down on the Monte Oro landing strip and now taking off again? I hadn't heard any plane land. Gabe crossed to the window. Listened.

"Boss! It's the other Beechcraft!"

Hardin walked to the window. They both looked and listened, peered through the dark night toward the fire that had crept closer down the slopes, and the shadows of men and machines battling to save the estate. For an instant, no one watched me.

Out the door I ran along the marble corridor and across the rotunda, alert for Lovat. Through the kitchen and down the dim servants' corridor, I saw no sign of the butler or anyone else. My rented car still stood in front of the garages. I got my little Colt Agent from under the seat. Gabe ran out the side door. I fired once. He dove back inside.

In the car I drove down the gravel drive toward the sound of the engines. Gabe reappeared in the doorway with Hardin behind him. I drove around the corner of the house and lost sight of them. Outside the house the powerful sound of the aircraft engines was louder and closer in the night that flickered with the light of the fire on the slopes.

Behind the massive villa the gravel drive forked. The landing strip was down the left fork through the trees and beyond the polo field. A car was coming behind me. I saw the stone storeroom where Gabe and Harry had locked me up while they consulted with Hardin. The sound of the engines was directly ahead and moving away from me. The other car was still behind me, and far off beyond the big house I heard the faint rising wail of a siren.

As I emerged from the trees and had a clear view of the landing strip, the roar of the aircraft engines rose higher and higher. At the far end of the strip, a second Beechcraft shook and shuddered as it revved up, poised for takeoff. I drove on past the stone storeroom, saw the small green Honda parked in front of it, and saw I would be too late.

The Beechcraft began its takeoff.

I stopped and got out of the car. The plane rolled down the black runway, guided by the encroaching glow of the fire that moved relentlessly down the mountains on the hot canyon winds.

Behind me the pursuing car emerged from the trees. It, too, stopped. Hardin and Gabe got out. The Beechcraft gathered speed. The siren had reached the house back beyond the trees and gone silent. It would be far too late. The Beechcraft swept down the macadam strip parallel to the burning mountains, swept on toward the far end, the dark sky, and, probably, Mexico to the south. Mexico and escape.

Then I saw her.

She stood in the middle of the dark runway, outlined by the flames now just beyond the walls of the estate. She held a pistol out in front of her in both hands. The Beechcraft was almost on top of her. I saw the pistol jump and buck. There was no sound, until, like an echo, the reports came faint across the darkness above the roar of the Beechcraft's engines. Nine faint explosions, one after the other, steadily, straight at the plane. Then it was up and over, airborne and flying away into the darkness.

J.C. Connors, the empty pistol hanging loose in her hand, stood alone on the runway and watched the Beechcraft gain altitude like some dark bird illuminated by the light of the burning mountains. I ran out toward her. Gabe and Hardin walked up behind me.

The fire glow shadowed J.C. Connor's face. "She killed Doreen. Pushed her over that cliff. Got her drugged on barbiturates and pushed her over. Just like that."

"You went to Hermosa Beach?"

She nodded. "I saw her drive out alone, had to follow her." She raised her eyes to the Beechcraft, which had turned now toward the mountains and the south. "I heard Drake laugh, tell her he had proof. Then she shot him. She shot Brownlee. I screamed. It scared her, and she ran out a back way to her car. I lost her again, so I came up here, got in through the wall the way you did the other day. I saw her come out of the house, but she drove away before I could reach her. All I could do was run after her. The plane was already on the runway. She was escaping. Free. Alive."

She went on staring up at the Beechcraft.

The plane coughed.

Hardin and Gabe had reached us from their car. They stared up at the plane, which seemed to hesitate. Sputter.

"Jesus!" Gabe said.

Hardin only looked up into the dark sky made bright by the flames. The engine coughed, missed. At the house the distant siren growled into life again and moved toward us.

The Beechcraft began to turn. Back toward the runway, the estate. The illusion of safety.

"No!" I said aloud. To the sky. To nothing.

The natural instinct. To turn for the haven of home, of the earth, of the familiar. A fatal instinct.

The struggling engine stalled.

The plane never completed its turn. Tilted and half-turned, it plunged straight into the smoke and glow of the sweeping fire. A pillar of fire mounted high into the dark sky.

"Christ," Gabe said.

I took the pistol from J.C. Connors. "Go home. There's no way to know if you hit the engine or not. She shouldn't have turned. She was running from two murders. I used the gun."

"You don't have to protect me. I hope I killed her."

"No, you don't, not really. Go home."

She watched me, then walked off into the darkness, followed by the eerie glow of the great fire. Hate now, hate and revenge. The tears would come later. Tears for her dead daughter, for all girls dead too soon. Her mission of search, of retribution, had been, really, to keep Doreen alive, to make Doreen go on living if only in her mother's mind. Now it was over. Now Doreen was really dead. Gone forever. Now J.C. Connors would have to face that. Now she would cry.

The siren had reached the far edge of the landing strip. I wiped the gun, held it in my hand. If it was registered to her, I'd tell them I had taken it from her earlier. Hardin was still staring up at the empty sky as if the Beechcraft were still there, still flying, escaping.

The sweeping glow of the fire glistened on the sweat of all our faces. Hardin, Gabe, and myself.

I said, "Maybe she hit the plane, maybe not. I'll make a deal. I fired at it, tried to stop Norma Powell, and I say nothing about Jay Norca, Duncan Stone, or my kidnapping."

Gabe watched Hardin in the flickering light.

"I would have gotten her off," Hardin said. "No matter what she'd done." He was staring at the place where Norma Powell had vanished in her own firestorm, and there was something a lot like tears in his eyes. "I could have gotten her off no matter what, damn her! Drake was a blackmailer and no one alive saw her push that damned girl off the cliff. I could have put the money, the power, in the right places. That's what it's for. I could have saved her. At worst a slap on the wrist." He looked at me. An old man. Beaten. "I would have saved her, Shaw. She panicked. She ran. Why? Why?"

"Because she couldn't really think of anyone except herself, and couldn't believe anyone else could. Once you knew about Doreen Connors and Drake, she couldn't trust you—even you—not to think of yourself first, throw her to the wolves."

The police car had stopped, and the sheriff walked slowly toward us, a deputy behind him. The sheriff himself. This was Walter Maxwell Hardin's estate. The sheriff was torn and dirty, his uniform soaked with sweat, dirt and ashes.

"What a waste," Hardin said, still staring at the fire where her plane had exploded. "What a stupid, stupid waste."

He meant what a waste of something he should have had, owned, enjoyed. Something he had needed and would not now ever have. A willful, wasteful denial of his need. Of him.

The sheriff touched his cap in salute to Hardin, turned to look at me. His face was drained, exhausted. The deputy stood behind and to the left with his gun out. The deputy was neat and clean, out from the office.

"You Paul Shaw? Captain Jacoby down in Hermosa Beach called us, asked us to look for you and a Norma Powell out here at Mr. Hardin's place about a murder down his way. You want to tell me about it?"

I told him. I left out who killed Jay Norca, Duncan Stone's beating, my kidnapping. It was my offer to Hardin: J.C. Connors for him and his musclemen. Duncan would heal, Jay Norca has been no loss, I hadn't been hurt, and Hardin would suffer enough without Norma Powell. J.C. Connors was worth the deal.

Hardin said nothing. Not even when I told the sheriff about Norma Powell and his campaign to save her. Norma was dead. There was no advantage to turning J.C. Connors in. He would rather look like an old fool, save himself and his muscle for new power plays in the future.

FORTY-FIVE

I SAT IN Sandra Peterson's small living room. In the early-morning hours few lights broke the night of the city. The fire in Santa Monica was out now, the distant flames in the San Gabriels all but vanished. Farther to the north, where the fires had seared us all, they were still battling. They would save Hardin's mansion, all the mansions, and they would turn back the fires once more. Until the next time.

They took us to the sheriff's office for our statements. Hardin and Gabe got the red carpet and kid gloves. It's their county. With the fire on everyone's hands, they got around to me about eleven, let me go by midnight. I stopped in Ventura, but J.C. had already checked out, gone back to New York.

We were drinking beer. It tasted cool and wet.

"She'll cry a long time," Sandra said. "It must be horrible, your child murdered. I don't think I could face it."

"Worse than a husband?"

"Yes," she said. She drank her beer and looked around the small room with its secondhand furniture and orange crates. "We were only married a year."

She seemed to be trying to remember that year in the furniture and air of the small living room, the high view with its few scattered lights. She hadn't looked at the bedroom yet. Neither had I.

"Jay Norca killed him. Pointer is boasting about it up in Folsom. Nobody makes an asshole out of Jack Pointer." I drank the cold, cold beer. "I think Robbie read the articles and spotted Norca and the police told him about Doreen's death and it all scared him. The jury would think he was the leader and crucify him, and Norca was out to kill all of them, so he came to me for help. Only Norca found him first."

She got up and brought us two more beers. Sat down again on the old couch facing me, her legs curled up under her purple terrycloth robe, her long dark hair loose now. Her real hair.

"Could he have gotten her off?" she said. "Hardin?"

"Probably. Money can do almost anything in this country. If the trouble doesn't become too public, there isn't even any 'almost.' Money and power can fix everything."

She nodded, more to herself than to me, and then she looked toward the bedroom. I had my tie off, nothing else. I didn't look at the bedroom.

"Brownlee's out of danger and talking," I said. "The sheriff told me what Jacoby in Hermosa Beach told him. After she'd found out from Pointer where the pills were and told Drake and Norma, Doreen Connors got so scared she tried to call the whole deal off. Scared of Pointer, scared the four would blow it and Pointer would find out and come after her. She threatened to tell Pointer. She was hysterical. Pointer had had her scared so long she just came apart. Got high on barbiturates.

"Norma got more Seconal and drove off with her in Doreen's car. Drake followed them up into the Angeles Forest, saw them walk to the edge of the cliff. Doreen was out on her feet, Norma pushed her over. Only Doreen grabbed Norma's shirt and ripped off the sleeve. Norma must have gotten something from Doreen's car on her sandals, too. She walked out of the forest, but stopped to bury her shirt, sandals, and the Seconal pill bottle.

"Drake dug them up. When the scam went bust and Norma got close to Hardin, Drake saw his chance to pull the blackmail. He laid low until Norca got killed and it looked like just the right time. He told Norma he wanted two hundred and fifty thousand for each of them. She said okay, where was the evidence? Drake laughed, told her he didn't have it in that apartment, money first. Instead she shot both of them. She'd have killed Brownlee, but J.C. Connors screamed and Norma ran. She was in the mansion, heard me tell Hardin the story. She figured the game was up and made her escape.''

Sandra drank, watched the distant dark hills across her canyon. ''She should have trusted Hardin.''

''She was never taught to trust,'' I said. ''Only herself. Her own needs, self-interest. She and Hardin.''

Sandra looked at the bedroom again. At me. I drank. What did I need? Want?

''I went to Malibu, and to the rooming house,'' Sandra said. ''Your friend Stone is up and walking around. He'll need some plastic surgery later, but he's all right. He wants the story exclusively.''

''How are the Hartmanns?'' I said.

''The old woman's going to be okay, but they won't be the same. They're broken inside. Afraid. They'll rent only to older people with good references and keep their doors locked. They won't go out at night anymore. Soon they probably won't go out at all.'' She drank. ''Is the good in people destroyed by other people?''

''Usually,'' I said.

I got up and went to her and carried her into the bedroom. She rested her head against my shoulder. I took off her robe, undressed. She watched me from the bed.

''Paul?''

''Go ahead,'' I said. ''Say it.''

She shook her head. ''I can't put it into words. The right words.''

''Don't worry about the right words. You mean you're afraid I won't like the right words. Never mind me. Just say the real words.''

She looked at me. "I want you, but I want to be alone. Me and Garbo. I want you to come to Los Angeles often. I want you to call me and come to the apartment and stay with me and then go back to New York. I want to keep you, but I don't want to own you." She looked away. "I don't want you to own me. I don't want anyone to own me."

"All right."

She looked back at me. "What?"

"All right. I understand."

"You understand? Tell me then."

"I'll come out here when I can. I'll call you. I'll come up to your apartment. I'll go back to New York and my wife. As long as it lasts that way, that's what I'll do."

"How long will it last that way?"

"How do I know? A week maybe. Ten years."

"Wait and see?"

"Wait and see."

She smiled. "I'll drink to that."

"I'll come out as often as I can," I said.

"I'll be here," she said.

What kind of marriage you have, what kind of life, depends on the circumstances of your life, on who you become. On what you come to need. Norma Powell had had her needs, Hardin his. And I had mine.

"British espionage at its best..."
—New York Times Book Review

murder
of a
moderate
man JOHN
HOWLETT

A trail of terror leads an Interpol operative to London and Milan
where he must untangle a web of deceit that surrounds an Iran-
ian opposition leader who is stalked by assassins.

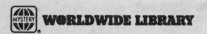

Take 2 books & a surprise gift FREE

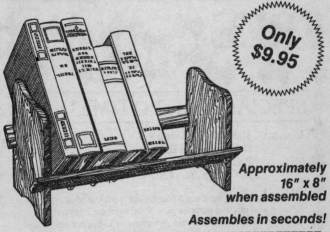